Also by Joe Corso

The Time Portal Series
The Old Man and the King
The Starlight Club Series
The Revenge of John W
The Adventures of the Lone Jack Kid
The Comeback
Engine 24: Fire Stories

LAFITTE'S TREASURE

By Joe Corso

Lafitte's Treasure
Joe Corso
Copyright 2014 by Joe Corso

Published by
Black Horse Publishing
Cover Art by Marina Shipova
Formatting by BZHercules.com

Black Horse Publishing
www.blackhorsepublishing.com

"He left a corsair's name to other times. Linked one virtue to a thousand crimes."
Lord Byron
(The last line in his poem, "The Corsair")

Table of Contents

Prologue

1814 New Orleans, Louisiana

It was a bright, sunny day outside, but inside the Old Absinthe House was cast in a dusk-like cozy darkness. Lamps secured to beams produced light, which cast an eerie amber glow that flickered and danced along the walls like a chorus of silent ballerinas. The bartender remained busy behind the long bar, cleaning the bar top and getting the place ready for the crowd he knew would come in later in the day. But he kept his eye on the table where four men sat in a darkened corner away from prying eyes, and far enough away that their voices couldn't be heard. This was an important meeting for both the general and New Orleans, and possibly for the United States. The Old Absinthe House was carefully chosen for this encounter because it was considered a safe place to meet for the two men who didn't know one another well enough yet to trust; and safety was, after all, the primary concern.

In the days prior to the meeting, and on a number of different occasions, Governor Claiborne had been poisoning General Jackson's mind on just what type of man he would be meeting. At first, because of Claiborne's harping, Jackson denounced Lafitte and his men as "Hellish Banditti," and he stubbornly refused to meet with the pirate. Lafitte, having had no success in convincing Governor Claiborne of the imminent attack by the British, attempted instead to meet directly with General Jackson.

Lafitte wrote Jackson that he had important information about the British plans to attack New Orleans, but Jackson had turned down Lafitte's request for a meeting; not once, but twice. After reading Lafitte's latest letter, Jackson refused to meet with him yet a third time. The question Jackson kept asking himself, after reading the communication, was "can I trust this man?" But he dismissed the question and made up his mind not to respond to Lafitte's latest request for a meeting. He would never lower himself to meet with a common pirate.

When Lafitte received the news that Jackson once again wouldn't meet with him, he tried a different approach. The following day, a letter was delivered to General Jackson by the Reverend Abbe Dubourg of the First St. Louis Cathedral. After reading the note, the general changed his mind. It was a simple letter stating that war with Britain was imminent and that Jackson, having no money and little in the way of arms, was ill-prepared to fight this war. The writer went on to assure Jackson that he could help him with both money and arms. It was signed "Jean Lafitte." But neither the letter itself, nor the message it contained, was what changed Jackson's mind about agreeing to attend the meeting. It was the little symbol under Lafitte's name that convinced him to attend.

Jackson was reassured when he shook Lafitte's hand. Jackson gave, and received in return, the grip of a Master

Mason. Feeling a little more comfortable now, he sat beside his aide, Lieutenant Andrew Ross, who commanded the 7th Infantry. Lafitte was accompanied by his brother, Dominique Youx, who sat beside him at the table. Lafitte spoke French and Spanish, as well as perfect English, which he opted to speak for this meeting.

Lafitte motioned to the bartender, who had been waiting for a signal to bring to the table the special cognac that was kept high above the bar for special occasions such as this. "I have a treat for you, *mon général*. A special brandy such as you have never tasted."

"I thought we were going to have a meeting," Jackson said caustically.

Lafitte acted as if he hadn't heard Jackson's brusque answer. "But of course we are. However, first we drink to celebrate our new partnership before we talk business," he said with a hint of a smile.

"Our new partnership? You're being a little presumptuous, aren't you?"

"Not at all, General, as you shall see. But first, we drink, and then I'll explain everything to you . . . and then you will understand."

Although Lafitte trusted André, the bartender and owner of the establishment, to keep his mouth shut, he remained quiet until André left, knowing the general would feel uncomfortable discussing business in front of a stranger. The general, who frequently enjoyed a glass of good whiskey, savored the drink, commenting on how delightful the cognac was, which pleased Lafitte, and he poured another round.

After downing his drink, Lafitte brushed his mustache lightly with the tip of his finger. "Now we talk business. The reason I wanted to meet with you was to tell you what I discovered of the British plans to attack New Orleans. A few weeks ago, a British warship sailed into our harbor and fired a warning shot. Some of my men and I rowed out to see what they wanted, and a meeting ensued under a British flag of truce. Captain Nicholas Lockyer, the commander of the *Sophie*, confided in me that he had been ordered to contact the commandant at Barataria. Since we were on the water and I could have easily been captured, I didn't say anything. Once we were safely on shore, I informed Lockyer that I was the commandant and I invited him and his men to dine with me at my home, which was built on the highest point on the island, so I could see what ships approached the island. I call the house 'Maison Rouge' because of its bright red color. During dinner, I asked Lockyer what his purpose was in seeking me out, and that's when he handed me a sealed document that explained in detail the British offer to me." Lafitte laughed. "You know, I had a hell of a time convincing my men not to hang the Brits."

Jackson cast him a sidelong glance. "Why did you stop your men from hanging them?"

"I overruled them because the British came seeking me under a flag of truce and I insisted that it be honored."

Jackson was curious about the offer. "What exactly did the British offer you?"

"Their offer was quite generous, *mon général*. They offered me a captaincy in their navy, and property guaranteed to me and my men, including a bonus of 30,000 pounds in gold, which would be given to me if I joined the British and fought against the Americans."

"So why didn't you accept their offer?" Jackson interrupted him to ask.

Before answering the question, Lafitte hesitated and looked at Ross, and then his gaze returned to the general. "Is your lieutenant a traveling man?" he asked.

Jackson smiled and nodded. "Yes. We are both members

of St. Tammany Lodge No. 1 of free and accepted Masons in Nashville, Tennessee."

"Good; as are my brothers and I. Now we can talk freely. We, as Freemasons, as you well know, will never take up arms against our country. God and our country come before all else. What I propose, General, is that since we are like-minded, we join forces. When I offered to tell Claiborne what I knew about the British plans to attack New Orleans, I had ten ships that I was prepared to offer you to use as you saw fit. But instead, that pig of a governor ordered Commodore David Porter, who is in charge of the navy here in New Orleans, to attack my base, arrest my brothers and me, and confiscate all my ships. Porter was happy to comply with the governor's orders because he stood to receive one-quarter of everything that was sold, and that included my ships. Claiborne is an egotistical, self-centered bastard, who used the navy to attack my base, steal my ships, confiscate my cargo, and imprison my brother Pierre. Luckily, Dominique and I got wind of his plans and disappeared before he could find us, but I didn't have time to warn my brother Pierre and my men."

Jackson thought back to the conversations he had with Governor Claiborne and nodded. "Now it all makes sense. You made it easy for Claiborne when you came to see him. All he had to do to defeat the notorious Lafitte brothers was to have you and your men arrested—and once you were out of the way, he could then legally steal everything you own."

"That's right, *mon ami*, except he didn't capture Dominique and me, and we still have two ships for you to use against the British. It's too bad, because you could have had ten ships. The Americans took custody of six of my schooners, one felucca, and a brig, as well as twenty cannon and cargo worth half a million dollars. Now tell me, General, what is it that you absolutely must have to fight this war that I might be able to assist you with? You have men, no?"

"Men are still reporting in. I expect a militia from Tennessee to arrive sometime today with 800 men, and I estimate that I'll have approximately 5000 men in total to fight the war, while the British will have at least twice and maybe three times that number. Some in power have even heard rumors that they may field as many as 25,000 men against us." Jackson looked at Lafitte and ground his teeth. "It's hopeless. How do they expect me to win this war with the little I have to fight it with?"

"Why do you say you can't win the war with what you have, my friend?" Lafitte asked.

Jackson looked at him with a shadow of a smile on his face and shrugged. "It's simple. Because I don't have the ammunition with which to fight the war."

"Ahh, but, General, I have all the ammunition you need, and it is yours, and I will be happy to give it to you."

Jackson's eyes lit up. "You have ammunition?"

"Yes!"

"Enough ammunition for all 5000 of my men?" he asked incredulously.

"Yes, and cannons and cannonballs and the two best cannoneers any general could hope for. Renato Beluche, an ex-commander of mine, and my brother Dominique, who is better than all of your cannoneers put together—he's even better than Beluche and Beluche is considered one of the best cannoneers to sail the seas . . . and they both are yours to use as you see fit. All you have to do is point them at the enemy and warn your officers not to interfere with them while they are at work."

Dominique's face turned crimson at the compliment. He was a short, muscular man with very wide shoulders and he was strong as a bull, but his most esteemed quality was his ability to hit whatever he aimed his cannon at.

"Your offer of ammunition will certainly help, but I still need money, plenty of money to feed and house my men, as well as buy horses, saddles, rifles, and uniforms for them. God knows how long this war will last and I don't have the time to go back to Washington to try to raise the money."

Jean Lafitte absently stroked his beard as he thought about this. "How much money do you need, *mon général*?"

"About one million dollars."

"*Sacre bleu*, but that is a lot of money . . . I have that much and more, but it is not in cash; it is in merchandise. But don't worry. Leave everything to me and I will get you the money to fight your war. You concentrate on organizing your army and let me worry about the money." Lafitte leaned over the table and looked directly into Jackson's eyes. "General, I want your word that if I make good on my promises and deliver what I say I will, and my brothers and I help you defeat the British, I want you to agree to have all my men pardoned of all and any crimes they have been charged with. And I want my brother Pierre released from prison immediately."

Jackson didn't have to think about Lafitte's request; he agreed to it without hesitation. He was surprised to find that he liked this pirate in spite of his earlier reservations. He was young—about thirty-two years of age—intelligent, graceful, and elegant in the manner in which he comported himself, and he dressed like a sophisticated gentleman. Jackson was impressed with how surprisingly accomplished he was in conversation. And yet this was the man that Governor Claiborne described as the murderous, ferocious leader of "pirates and desperadoes." General Andrew Jackson prided himself on being a good judge of people and this man was nothing like the man the governor described to him. Jackson leaned over the table to Lafitte. "I don't know if you are aware of this, but the governor has issued a reward of $500 for you, dead or alive."

Lafitte's eyebrows lifted a little and he smiled mischievously. "I have heard the same thing, my friend. I know about the $500 reward the governor has placed on my head and, in return, I have placed a $5000 bounty, dead or alive, on the governor's head."

They both laughed, and Jackson found that he enjoyed being among real men. He was deriving pleasure from this conversation. At the moment, he wasn't in any hurry to leave. Besides, the cognac was good and he was having too good a time to part company with these men.

"Another drink, General, to celebrate our partnership and to defeating the British." Another series of rounds was poured as the four men continued to discuss and formulate their plans.

When the general and his aide were about to leave, Lafitte took him gently by the arm. "General, I'm speaking to you on the square. I will help you up to the length of my cable tow." The general understood the Masonic significance of what Lafitte said and nodded.

"That's all a man and a Mason could ask for," the general said as he turned to leave.

"Don't forget, General," Lafitte called out. "My brother. Don't forget to have Pierre released from prison as soon as possible."

The general mounted his horse but, before riding off, he turned his horse, leaned over close to Lafitte and told him, "You have my word. As soon as I get back to my headquarters, I will give the order for your brother's release and he will join you no later than two days from now."

***

Lafitte spent the next few days organizing a meeting that would include all the landowners of New Orleans. He planned to set the meeting to take place two weeks from this coming Sunday at noon—and the meeting would be held deep in the bayous where his ships docked to unload their cargo. Lafitte had over 100 men under his command and he gave each man a list of names and sent them out with fast horses. They were charged with finding people and telling them it was important they attend this meeting. When Governor Claiborne learned of the meeting, he sent his spy, Raul Gaspanoux, down to the French Quarter. The governor and his contacts made sure Gaspanoux would be attending the meeting.

Everyone in New Orleans knew that a war with Britain was imminent. It could start within a few days, and certainly no more than a few months. Knowing this, every landowner within sixty miles of the bayou showed up for the meeting. They were curious, especially since they had nothing to offer him. They had no money and they weren't soldiers. While waiting for the meeting to begin, they found the tables laden with fine food and drink that Lafitte's cooks had prepared for them. They helped themselves and indulged in satisfying their appetites.

Lafitte had been on board his ship, the *Pride,* since early morning, but he preferred not to make his presence known until just before the start of the meeting. At exactly five minutes before noon, Lafitte walked down from his ship and greeted a few old friends before calling the meeting to order at exactly noon. The people standing before him were his friends, and even though he might not have known all of them, his fame was such that they all knew of him. Lafitte stood and waved both hands to get the crowd's attention, waiting a moment for the chatter to quiet down. Then he spoke. "Thank you for coming, my friends. I know you are all wondering why I asked you here today. I had a meeting with General Andrew Jackson two weeks ago and told him that the English had sent Captain Lockyer, an envoy, to see me. Over dinner, the captain handed me a sealed packet and, to my surprise, when I opened it I discovered that England had offered me a captaincy in their navy, as well as land for me and my men, and a bonus to me of 30,000 pounds in gold if I would join them to fight the United States."

"What did you do, Jean Paul? Did you take them up on their offer?" yelled a member of the crowd.

Lafitte gave him a dark look then smiled broadly. "Maybe I should have taken the gold and then gone to see General Jackson. That would be a good idea, no?"

Everyone laughed. Lafitte raised his hands once again to get their attention and quieten them down. "Let me tell you about our governor. As soon as the British envoy left, I contacted Governor Claiborne and asked for a meeting with him. I said I had information that General Jackson must be told ... and yet, when I went to the governor to tell him of the British plans, he used my offer to help New Orleans as an excuse to confiscate my ships and arrest my men." Lafitte raised his voice, rousing the crowd, and waved his arms until his face reddened from the exertion of shouting at the top of his lungs. "Governor Claiborne is a thief who stole my ships and cargo. Ships that could have been used by General Jackson to fight the British. And besides confiscating my ships, he arrested my men."

Someone in the crowd yelled out to Lafitte, "But why are we here? What do you need from us?"

"Ahh." Lafitte sighed. "What do I need from you? That's a very good question, my friend. What do I need from you? Well, it's not what I need from you; it's what General Jackson needs from you. General Andrew Jackson needs a million dollars to supply his troops with clothing, weapons, housing, food, uniforms, and manpower."

"But where will this money come from?" someone from

the crowd asked.

Lafitte pointed at the crowd. "From you, and you, and you."

The crowd was confused because, in their wildest dreams, they knew they could they never accumulate that much money.

Another landowner yelled out, "What do you mean? Explain yourself."

Lafitte asked for a show of hands of how many had their property paid for in full. About thirty percent raised their hands. "How many of you hold mortgages?" The rest all raised their hands. "I want each of you to bring me the deeds to your property so I can use the equity in your property to borrow money from the banks. I will personally cover all your notes. I have cargo worth much more than the million dollars that Jackson needs, but it is not liquid and, with the war looming on the horizon, I don't have the time to convert my assets into cash. What's more, if the British win the war, your property will become worthless. I need the deeds to your property for collateral in order to obtain money to finance the war. You have nothing to fear, because I will, as I said before, back the debt with my personal wealth. Now, I want all of you to go home and return here no later than tomorrow with the deeds to your property. In the meantime, while I'm waiting for your deeds, I will negotiate with the banks—and I will not touch any of the money. My part is to negotiate with the banks and they themselves will deliver the money to General Jackson. I do not do this for myself and, I repeat, none of the money will ever be touched by me. I do this for New Orleans and for the Untied States of America."

As soon as the meeting ended, Gaspanoux, the governor's spy, mounted his horse and sped away.

The following day, all the deeds to all the property in New Orleans were in the possession of Jean Lafitte. Five banks located in and around New Orleans approved the loan. They agreed to give General Jackson a letter of credit totaling one million dollars to be used by Jackson in the upcoming war.

Lafitte showed a letter from General Jackson to the banks attesting to the fact that Lafitte's property, which had been confiscated by Governor Claiborne, would be returned to Lafitte upon the conclusion of the war. Lafitte assured the banks in front of a notary that the deeds would guarantee that the loan would be paid in case his property was not returned or was somehow lost in transit. Thus, Lafitte was allowed to keep the deeds in his possession.

What Lafitte intended to do now required people he trusted—his Masonic brothers. The only one he could think of to do what he had in mind was his friend and brother Mason, and sometime pirate, Barthelemy Lafon. He took his brother Dominique Youx aside and instructed him to go to Lafon's home. If he wasn't there he was to go to his office, find him, and tell him to report to the blacksmith's shop immediately. What Lafitte had to tell him could not wait.

Dominique found Lafon at home and gave him his brother's message. Without wasting any time, Lafon and Dominique got on their horses and rushed to Jean's blacksmith shop.

Lafon was a noted New Orleans architect and his services included map-making, planning the design for Donaldsonville in 1806 and surveying and making recommendations for improvements to the fortifications of New Orleans. He was also a friend of the Lafittes and a part time privateer.

The two men embraced and Lafon didn't waste words. "What can I do for you, my friend?"

Lafitte pointed to a table with a bottle on it. "Come; let's sit down and talk over a tankard of rum." Lafitte poured two drinks then lifted his tankard to his friend and made a toast.

"Here's to a successful conclusion to the war." Then he put his drink on the table. "I wish I knew how this war would end, Bart, but I don't have a clue. So just in case it doesn't go in our favor—and this is between you and me—I'm going to hide a treasure. I intend to create a series of clues. Then I'll hide the treasure and, if I don't retrieve it, it won't be found until sometime in the future."

Lafon was intrigued. "But, what do you want me to do, Jean?"

Jean took a deep swig of the rum and leaned forward. "As you already know, I have all the deeds to the properties in New Orleans, but if we lose the war I don't want the British to get their hands on them. I spoke to Joseph LePorte, the prior of the First St. Louis Cathedral, and told him I would contact him shortly with an important service he must do for me. I warned him that our meetings and discussions were to be kept secret, and he agreed to help us. What I want you to do is go to the First St. Louis cemetery and locate a tomb, a very specific tomb. Find the tomb of the widow's son and create a false façade with a Masonic symbol on it. Place it high on the tomb, because that is where I will place one of the clues. I intend to create a riddle that only the person who can follow the clues will be able to use to find the treasure."

"Treasure? Of course, you mean the deeds. Am I correct?"

"Yes and no. It is true that I intend to hide the deeds, but I also want to include some of the jewels I've collected through the years. Look, my friend, everyone assumes I've hidden treasure in various places and they would be right, but war is about to begin, and the part of my treasure that has not been buried has to be hidden with the deeds. I don't want the British to find them. Find me that tomb and design a hollow brick or façade. Simply use your imagination. When it's completed, show it to me."

Chapter 1

Present

The company was preparing to fight a roaring fire at the end of an old rusted hulk of a pier on the West Side of Manhattan that looked like part of a set of an old Frankenstein movie.

"What do you think, Eddie?" Since Eddie was the senior man, Lieutenant Chafey sometimes asked for his opinion, and this was one of those times.

"I think we should wait for the boats. They should be here in a few minutes and they can do in minutes what it will take us hours to do. Besides, there's no life at risk on this empty, rotting pier. In fact, we would be doing the city of New York a favor by letting it burn down. Let's set up a multiversal nozzle and pour water on it from here. You asked for my opinion and, for what it's worth, I just gave it to you."

Two of the guys wanted to take the hose line out to where the fire was eating away part of the pier, taking a position on the far end of the pier opposite the fire and pouring water on it from there.

"Okay, let's move the line onto the pier," ordered Lieutenant Chafey. When you're part of a squad or unit, you do things in a group you would never do alone, and this, again, was one of those times. Eddie was the senior man and he had the nozzle. The five members of his company, which included Eddie, pulled hose and stretched the line to a position at the end of the pier, near but opposite to the fire. Getting into position was not easy because the pier was in a terrible state of decomposition. There were holes everywhere in the timbers covering the center of the pier, so the company had to be careful. One false step and someone could fall through the rotten wooden into the icy waters of the Hudson River. Being a pier company, the men never pulled their boots up; they always kept them down, because if they fell into the water with their boots pulled up, they would sink like an anchor. So, with their boots down, they moved the line into position.

The supporting structure of the pier was steel, but the rest of the pier was wood, so they had a hell of a fire to put out. They could hear the whistle coming from the boats in the distance, signaling they were on their way, but their ETA was still about seven or eight minutes. Eddie would rather have waited for them than be positioned at the end of this long ugly pier. But putting out fires was his job, and this was, after all, a fire that had to be put out.

The engine company always stretched three-and-a-half-inch hose at a pier fire with water supplied by their chauffeur, Charlie. However, all the hydrants had been sucked dry by other rigs also busy fighting the fire, so Charlie's only option was to draft water from the Hudson River. When their water came, Eddie bled the line and pulled back the controlling nozzle. As the water shot out, they started their attack on the fire. They really needed three or four lines attacking the fire from different positions to have any effect, but they did the best they could under the circumstances, knowing the boats would arrive shortly. Eddie worked a pier job once for two and a half hours, then the boats came and, in one minute, they knocked the pier down and put the fire out. That was why it didn't make much sense to Eddie for the company to be in this position. As soon as the boats arrived, they would have to shut their line down and back out, taking their hose line with them. This was double the work and, in Eddie's opinion, totally unnecessary.

The boats were closer now and he strained his eyes,

looking through the smoke to see from what direction they would be coming; but the smoke was very thick, making it all but impossible to see. Wind from the Hudson lifted the smoke for an instant and a fireboat appeared out of the haze, looming so close he could touch it. Just as the fireboat was about to open up with its powerful streams of water, it bumped into the pier and Eddie heard a groan. The eerie sound seemed to come from the very heart of the old pier when, suddenly, one side buckled and started to pitch into the river. The guys behind Eddie took off, running for their lives, leaving only him and Lieutenant Chafey on the line.

"Drop the line, Eddie," the lieutenant ordered. "We have to make a run for it before this old pier collapses under us." They dropped the hose line and ran as fast as safety permitted, careful not to fall through one of the large openings with which the old pier was riddled. Eddie was about halfway to safety when the boats opened up with their powerful multiple streams and the pier completely broke apart like a jigsaw puzzle that wasn't glued down. The end of the pier dropped like a chunk of ice into the cold Hudson River. Lieutenant Chafey made it to safety, but Eddie wasn't as lucky. As the pier dropped into the river, he lost his equilibrium and fell towards the water. His knee hit a steel beam and something snapped. Eddie knew he was hurt, but had no idea how bad it was. His only concern now was to stay alive. He'd worry about his knee later. Luckily, most of the pier had fallen below him, but he wasn't taking any chances because parts of the old pier were still falling around him. He slid off his boots and slipped out of his turnout coat, letting it fall to the bottom of the river. Strangely though, he held on to his helmet as he swam under the remaining part of the pier to the other side. Bumping into something, he felt a hook brush past his chest. He took hold of it as a hand grabbed his arm and pulled him out of the icy Hudson River.

Chapter 2

Julianna didn't mind the drive to and from work. It relaxed her. She played her Joe Cocker CD, the *Best of Joe Cocker*, the millennium collection, especially the song "You Are So Beautiful." She couldn't figure out how he could put that song over so beautifully with his craggy mournful voice. She actually enjoyed going to work now that she had graduated and become a registered nurse. She loved her job. She had worked hard and hadn't had time for dates or socializing with friends. But when she got her new job at the hospital, she treated herself to a new wardrobe. She was twenty-six years old, with jet-black hair inherited from her French ancestors and a beautiful face highlighted by her green eyes. She knew she was very pretty by the heads that turned when she entered a room with her unintentionally sexy walk. Most women tried very hard to be sexy, but not Julianna. She didn't have to try. She was that rare woman from whom sex appeal oozed like water from a faucet; she couldn't help it and she was powerless to turn it off.

Since moving to Hawthorne Place off Route 50, each morning she would drive to the hospital. Her car seemed to drive itself to work as if on autopilot. But today was different. Her mother had called this morning and asked Julianna to stop by when she got a free moment. She had discovered some papers in an old sea trunk and wanted Julianna to look through them before she threw anything out. They looked important but she didn't understand any of it. Julianna said she'd stop by over the weekend and take a look. Tonight, though, she had a date. She hadn't dated in months and was looking forward to going out. She didn't care what her date looked like. She just planned on having a good time. She wanted to shake off the months of studying and, for one night, be carefree and a little reckless and just enjoy herself. She deserved it.

Her mother agreed. "It's about time you went out on a date with a young man and enjoyed yourself."

As soon as Julianna arrived her mother took her by the arm. "Julianna, come upstairs with me. I have something to show you." They walked up to the second floor. Her mother pulled the attic access ladder from the ceiling and they took the steps slowly, until they were standing in the attic crawl space. "I haven't been up here in many years, honey. I don't know what possessed me to visit this old attic, but I did. I came upon this old sea chest that used to belong to your great-great-great-grandfather on your father's side and, with a little effort, I opened it. You know your ancestor was Jean Lafitte's brother Pierre. Your father told me they not only sailed together, they were inseparable. Well, anyway, I came upon a few of his possessions. Who knows? Maybe they have some value." She pulled out an old a spyglass, one that could be pulled out in sections. It was in excellent condition and could be worth some money. Then she pulled out a variety of other items. Two flintlock matching pistols, probably worth a fortune, a sword with a silver scabbard, an old navy uniform, an old, battle worn American flag, a Masonic bible, and a diary.

"Mom, you had this stuff all these years and you didn't know it?"

"Yes, honey. Your father was the one related to Lafitte and he must have put the trunk way back here in the corner and covered it with a tarp. It never caught my eye in all the years, if ever I came up here."

"Leave everything here. I'll contact an appraiser and make an appointment for him to look these items over. But I'd like

Lafitte's Treasure

to take the diary home so I can browse through it, if you don't mind. Who knows, maybe it'll be interesting reading."

"Not at all, honey. You take whatever you want. After all, this is now all yours."

Julianna spent the next two nights reading the diary and, when she was finished, she read it again. It was exciting stuff. The diary alone had to be worth a fortune if for only its historical value. It was a firsthand report of how Captain Lockyer, under orders from Lieutenant Colonel Nichols, offered Lafitte and his men a position in the English navy. Lafitte was to be made a captain and given a large tract of land. His men would be given land according to rank and, upon acceptance of this agreement, Jean Lafitte would turn over all of his war ships and his men to the British to augment their upcoming attack on New Orleans. When Lafitte didn't respond, they upped their offer. In addition to the rank of captain in the British Royal Navy and the extensive land grant they promised him, they would include a six thousand pounds sterling payment at his option. Lafitte asked for two weeks to consider it. He used the two weeks to make contact with Old Hickory, General Andrew Jackson. When the two weeks were up, Lafitte was approached for his acceptance of the British offer, which the British were certain he would accept. But, once again, Lafitte asked for two more days to consider their offer.

Captain Lockyer appeared off the Barataria Pass, awaiting the signal from Lafitte that he was willing to accept the offer made to him by Colonel Nichols. He was losing patience and when no answer was forthcoming, the brig finally sailed off. The British had exhausted their patience with Lafitte; or they figured they could no longer trust the man. The diary described the Battle of New Orleans in detail, and how Dominic Youx became a hero, using his cannon with great

25

accuracy while wounded. But it was the part about Lafitte hiding the clue to his treasure in his blacksmith shop that intrigued her. She read and re-read that part over and over, etching the words into her fertile mind.

She flew to New Orleans over the weekend and visited the Lafitte blacksmith shop, only to find it had been renovated in 1928. Checking the records, she found that a Pietro Calto had performed the renovations, and she set her mind to track down his descendants. She was sure the one who rebuilt the Lafitte shop was the one who found her treasure. She was determined to follow up on it and find the man who many years ago had taken the treasure she felt was rightfully hers.

Chapter 3

"How's your leg feel?"

"Hurts like hell, Doc. But it doesn't hurt as much as it did, and I can tell it's getting better every day." Of all the medical doctors that examined sick and injured firefighters, Eddie liked Dr. Robinson best because he cared for the men and, even though he worked for the city, did his best for all firefighters. The doctor was down to earth and the men related to him as if he was one of them. He was about fifteen years older than Eddie, in his late forties or early fifties. The doctor was a short, slim, balding man who wore his glasses low on his nose.

Dr. Robinson put down the file. "You know, the two consulting doctors the department referred you to suggested you have your knee operated on, which confirmed my own diagnosis. Are you going to get the operation?"

"Look, Doc. I have twelve years on the job and I'm still eight years short of my twenty, so it doesn't make any difference to me if I have to put in a few months of light duty. So yeah! I guess I will get the operation."

Dr. Robinson looked at Eddie for a long moment, as if deciding whether to take him into his confidence. He sighed, pulled his glasses further down his nose, looked over them into Eddie's eyes, and said. "Are you sure you want to have your knee operated on, son?"

Eddie narrowed his eyes. "Why are you asking me that? Are you trying to tell me something? Come on, Doc; talk to me."

Dr. Robinson sat back in his chair and removed his

glasses. "Because when they operate on your knee, son, they're going to dissect it. You know what you have, but you don't know what you're going to get."

Eddie asked him straight out, "Are you a surgeon?"

"Yes, I am, and my recommendation is that you should not get the operation. But that's just my opinion. You can get a second opinion and then make up your mind if you want the operation or not. The decision, of course, is yours to make. Your leg will heal in time, of that I'm sure. Although I wouldn't want you to carry me down a fire escape! But aside from that, your knee will heal just fine. If you decide to stay on the job, I'm afraid I'll have to recommend no more fire duty for you. But if you decide you're not going to get the operation, then I'm going to board you."

Eddie tilted his head. "What do you mean you're going to 'board' me? What does that mean?"

"You'll have to appear before a board, a medical board, for examination to confirm my diagnosis, prior to being discharged from the New York City Fire Department. If they put you off the job, you'll receive a three-quarter line-of-duty pension." Dr. Robinson smiled a knowing smile. "Of course, that means you won't get to appear on any more FDNY firefighter calendars."

Eddie smiled, displaying a perfect set of white teeth. "So you know about the calendar pictures, eh?"

The smile lingered a little longer on Dr. Robinson's face. "Sure I do. It's always nice to see a firefighter stay in shape; but now that you'll have all the time in the world, you better see to it that your body doesn't turn to fat."

"Do you know how much work I put into staying in shape, Doc? I work out at a dojo three times a week, and two other days I work out at a gym; or, if I'm working a tour, I'll work out in the firehouse for an hour. I try to put aside that hour a day to keep myself in shape. Except for the weekends when I relax, of course."

When Eddie left the medical office, he was shaken up. He had gone that morning for a routine medical follow-up visit, and when he left, his career as a firefighter was over. This was the only job he ever loved and it was over, finished, and he had no idea what he would do with the rest of his life.

Eddie returned to his home on 42nd Street, opposite Junior High School 16 in Corona, Queens. He stepped over an envelope that was pushed under the door, and went into the kitchen to put up a pot of coffee. He lived alone. His wife had left him ten years ago because she couldn't stand the uncertainty of being the wife of a firefighter. She never told him that was the reason, but he knew anyway when he came home from work one day and found all of her stuff gone. When she walked out the door, she walked out of his life. In the ten years since, he never heard from her again. Eddie tried calling her once, but her phone had been changed and her address was no longer current, so he put her out of his mind and went on with his life.

The delicious aroma of coffee wafted towards Eddie, and he poured himself a cup of Starbucks coffee and sat down at the kitchen table. He was feeling sorry for himself and the coffee had an uplifting effect. As he sipped his coffee, his eyes looked past the cup to the envelope. He walked over and picked it up, taking it to the table. He read the return address.

Epstein, Harris, and Jensen
Times Square Tower
7 Times Square
New York, NY 10036
Phone +1-555-326-2000

Eddie opened the envelope and read the letter.

Dear Mr. Calto,

The purpose of this letter is to arrange a meeting in our office at your earliest convenience to discuss the inheritance left to you by your great-great-grandfather, Pietro Calto. Please call me to set up an appointment.

Yours truly,

Thomas G. Carruthers, Partner
Epstein, Harris, and Jensen

Eddie did a quick Google search and found that Epstein, Harris, and Jensen was a prestigious Manhattan law firm with international offices in major countries, as well as branch offices sprinkled around America in major cities. One of the partners had taken the time to write this letter to him personally, to arrange an appointment.

When the phone was answered, Eddie asked for Mr. Carruthers and, after a few moments, a different woman's voice said, "Mr. Carruthers' office."

Eddie cleared his throat. "Mr. Carruthers, please. Ed Calto calling at his request for an appointment."

"Oh yes, Mr. Calto. I have your name on my priority list. I can handle the appointment for you, sir." She quickly checked Mr. Carruthers' schedule. "I have tomorrow morning at 10 a.m., or Tuesday at 2 p.m. Which would you prefer?"

"Tomorrow at ten is fine." She gave him instructions.

The following day, Eddie took a cab to 7 Times Square. He was using a crutch and didn't relish the thought of taking a bus or train, so a cab worked fine for him. He entered the building, took the elevator to the tenth floor and, when the doors opened, walked down the hall to his right as he had been instructed. He came to a large office with "T. CARRUTHERS, PARTNER" on the door. Inside, the secretary asked his name and who he was there to see. "Mr. Carruthers," Eddie said with a hint of a smile. She brushed back a lock of hair and smiled warmly. "Please have a seat while I tell Mr. Carruthers that his ten o'clock appointment is here."

Mr. Carruthers walked out from his office and introduced himself. Then he guided Eddie inside and offered him a seat opposite his desk, so that they were facing one another. Carruthers was a tall, athletic, good-looking man, and amiable in a serious way. Eddie glanced at the sumptuous office. There were golfing trophies on a shelf to the right of the door, and various laminated academic degrees and awards on the wall behind his desk from different fraternal organizations; but Eddie's eyes settled on an expensively framed picture of a beautiful woman on the corner of the desk. Next to it was another picture of two handsome boys and a pretty young girl, a younger version of the woman in the picture.

"Your family?" Eddie asked amiably.

"My wife, Linda." He looked at Eddie with a hint of pride. "And these are my sons and daughter."

"A beautiful family."

"Thank you." Then, the lawyer got right to the point. "Do you have any idea why I asked you to come here this morning, Mr. Calto?"

"No. Your letter was a surprise to me. I never knew my great-great-grandfather. He died way before I was born and I don't know much about him."

A thick open file lay on Mr. Carruthers' desk and he was silent while he read through the various clippings, picking up assorted snippets of papers with notes on them. Then, apparently satisfied with what he had read, he looked up from his file and began to explain why this meeting was necessary. "Your great-great-grandfather had something he felt was very important to him, and to you, and he wanted you to take possession of it on your thirty-fifth birthday. Your birthday was on February twenty-third, am I correct?"

"Yes."

The attorney took an envelope from the file folder. He opened it and turned it upside down. A key fell into his hand. "Your great-great-grandfather came to our California office on October 5, 1928 and left this key attached to this silk ribbon, which he insisted was to be placed permanently around your neck. That key and a teak box have been stored in our vault since that date, with instructions that we were to deliver the box to his eldest great-great-grandson on his thirty-fifth birthday. Since you are his only great-great-grandson, the box was to be given to you on or after your thirty-fifth birthday. I have no idea what is in the box, but I assume it must be some of his personal belongings. Why he chose this particular birthday, and why he skipped over your father, grandfather and great-grandfather to pass it on to you, I have no idea." The lawyer motioned for Eddie to approach his desk and sign the release on the line above his name. He then notarized his signature and told him that their business was just about concluded. "Except for one other item of importance, which I will get to in a moment."

Eddie scratched his head, confused. "Is there anything else you could tell me about my great-great-grandfather that would help me understand why he would leave me this box, in this manner, after all these years?"

"No, Mr. Calto. This box has been with our firm for the better part of a century and, at this moment, you know as much about it as I do. I can tell you this, though. Your great-great-grandfather, according to the agreement in my files, was in construction and, according to my notes, legend has it that he found something that changed him into a man of substance. He set up a trust fund with our company to defray the cost of storing the box with us for all these years—and the trust has grown. We have always taken our fee from the fund on a yearly basis at a figure your great-great-grandfather and our firm agreed to in 1928. But the balance of the trust fund has grown through the years and is now yours. I am having a check cut in your name as we speak in the amount of $1,275,000."

"WHAT? HOW MUCH?"

The lawyer smiled as he repeated the figure. Eddie had heard right, and he still couldn't believe it. His heart racing, he pictured himself taking an extended trip around the world, lounging on the white sands of some exotic beach, sipping a refreshing drink, and surrounded by bikini-clad girls, with no more worries. Sure enough, a few minutes later, the attorney's secretary walked into the office and handed the lawyer an envelope. He removed the check and corroborated the figure, then replaced it in the envelope and handed it to Eddie. "One other order of business. Your great-great-grandfather stipulated that the box was not to be opened at our office or in front of anyone. It was to be opened somewhere private when you were alone."

With their business concluded and the law firm having honored their contract, Eddie asked Mr. Carruthers if he could have his secretary arrange for a cab to pick him up in front of the building.

But Carruthers would have none of that. "I'll have our company executive limo take you to your bank. I'm sure you'll want to deposit your check first. Then our chauffeur will drive you home."

Chapter 4

Eddie held the satchel close to his chest as he stepped into the back seat of the big black stretch limo. As the limo pulled slowly away from the curb and assimilated itself into the heavy midtown traffic, another car that had been waiting for Eddie to leave the building pulled away from the curb and followed close behind.

The limo driver had noticed Eddie's Navy SEAL ring and, without turning his head, asked him, "How many years did you serve in the navy?"

Eddie, sat back in the plush seat. "Four years."

"Four years, eh? I was in for eight years myself. Should have stayed in for the term, but it seemed at the time like such a long time to go till retirement. Now that I look back, I should have stayed in the service. Would have been retired by now."

"Hey, I'm Eddie. Nice to meet you."

"Same here. I'm Al." Al pulled the big car to the curb in front of Eddie's bank. "Go on in and take care of business. I'll wait right here for you. If, when you come out, I'm not here, it means a cop told me to move and I had to drive around the block, so just wait a minute and I'll be back."

"Thanks, Al." Eddie strode into the recesses of the large bank, deposited the check and left. He was pleased to find Al and the limo still parked by the curb.

"Where to, Eddie?" Eddie gave Al his address and sat back, thinking about all that had happened today. This was a life-altering day. Al interrupted his thoughts. "Sorry, Al. I was deep in thought. What did you just say?"

"I didn't want to say anything before because I wasn't sure, but after I made the turn and parked by the bank, that car behind us did the same thing. It's been following us ever since I picked you up."

"I don't want to turn my head, Al. Could you turn the rear view mirror and tilt it so I could get a look at the guy?"

"Sure. How's that?"

"A little more to the right and down a little."

Al adjusted the mirror. "How is it now?"

"Perfect. Hmm, it's a black Mercedes. I wonder if it had anything to do with my visit to the lawyers today?"

Al shrugged. "I wouldn't know about that. Do you want me to try and lose him?"

Eddie thought for a moment then he made a decision. "No. Here's what we'll do. Instead of driving me home, drop me off in Long Island City under the El. I'll take the train to my stop. This guy may not want to leave a car in that neighborhood 'cause it may not be there when he gets back."

Al laughed. "Good thinking, Ed. Look. You seem like a nice guy. Here's my card. If you need me and if I can be of any help, call me."

Eddie took the card. "Gee, Al, that's very nice of you. I just might take you up on your offer."

Eddie took the train at the Rawson Street station for one exit. Then he hailed a cab, which he took to his home, always checking behind to see if he was being followed. It looked clear, so he told the driver to stop at the corner after going around the block twice. He paid the cab and walked tentatively toward his home. When he was sure he wasn't being followed, he slipped into his house. Once inside, he locked the door and, just to be safe, placed a chair under the doorknob. He opened the satchel, removed the teak box, and placed it on the kitchen table where he left it while he made a pot of coffee. He wanted to open the box but was afraid of what he would find. He sat in front of it, sipping his coffee. He used to drink it with cream and sugar, but they had run out of cream in the desert of Iraq, so he drank it black with sugar; but then the sugar ran out, so he drank the coffee black. Soon, not only did he get to enjoy the coffee, but he realized that by drinking it black, he could taste the actual flavor of the coffee. He had been drinking it black since then.

His eyes became glazed as he thought about all that had transpired this morning. If Al was right, the driver of the Mercedes must have been expecting him to appear at the bank this morning. *But how could they have known I would be going there? Unless my phones were tapped, or someone at the law firm notified the bad guys.* But that didn't seem logical. No! It had to be the phone. He thought back to the last time he had ATT service his phones. He remembered a time about two years ago when his line suddenly and without any reason went dead. He thought it strange at the time because the weather was good. There weren't any storms that could have interrupted the signal, so he attributed it to someone crashing their car into one of the utility poles. He was about to call the telephone company when there was a knock on the door. It was a telephone repairman. "Sorry to bother you," he said. "We've had a problem with the telephone lines and I'm checking to see if your lines were affected."

"Yes my phone line suddenly died and I was just about to call you guys."

"Let me check your line out. Do you mind if I come in?" A few minutes later, the phone line was working and the guy left, and Eddie forgot about it. Now that he thought about it, it was strange that the repairman asked to inspect all his phones. He had a phone in his kitchen, one in the living room, and one beside his bed, and the technician had examined all of them.

He rose from his chair, went over to the kitchen drawer, and pulled out a screwdriver. He picked up the phone and removed the bottom, which he remembered the repairman doing. Inside, he noticed a small, square silver card about the size of a postage stamp clipped to two tiny wires. He wasn't a telephone repairman, so he didn't know if that little plate was part of the phone or not. But it didn't look as though it belonged there, so he guessed this little gadget was bugging his phone. He had a cell phone, and he didn't think that was tapped, so he dialed his telephone service and told them that he wanted the phones removed. He gave the excuse that since he had a cell phone, he didn't need the added expense of a house phone. He was given an appointment for the following morning between 8 a.m. and twelve noon. He hoped whoever was listening to his phone conversations hadn't picked up that call. With that out of the way, he sat back down at the kitchen table and thought about his conversation with Al. He considered calling him, but changed his mind. There was little he could tell Al until he knew more.

Chapter 5

Eddie stared at the teak box on the kitchen table, with a knife in his hand, longer than he intended. He assumed his hesitation was only because he wanted the moment to linger, but something inside told him otherwise. He knew that as soon as he opened the box, reality would replace the anticipated treasures that the box concealed. Once Eddie opened the box, whatever trinkets his ancestor had left him would be visible and the alluring mystery of what could have been would no longer remain. So he remained quiet for a few moments longer, sitting with his wrist resting on the table and his knife facing straight up, pointing at the ceiling. He resembled a knight holding a lance before a joust. *Oh well*, he thought. *I might as well see what secrets the box holds.* He cut the three-inch strap encircling the box, removed the key from around his neck, placed it into the key slot, and turned it. There was an audible click as if a pressurized seal had been broken. Of course, it was just his imagination because there wasn't any such seal. Eddie lifted the cover and stared into the box. There was a removable dark blue velvet shelf that contained a letter addressed to him. He opened the letter and began to read.

October 5, 1928
To my great-great-grandson;
    Dear great-great-grandson, I apologize for not knowing your name and I guess it's only proper to apologize for having been dead the many years since this letter was written. I'm sorry I never lived to see you grow into the fine man I know you must be. I know you must be curious about why I have chosen to approach you in this manner. I could not leave this box with

your father or his father or his father's father, not because they weren't worthy of it, but because it was too soon, and too dangerous. The secret contained in this box is for your eyes only. Be careful not to tell anyone about what you will soon discover because it will put your life in danger. If you are careful, you will acquire and possess the riches of King Solomon. Let me start at the beginning.

Pharaohs of ancient times hired master masons to build their grand edifices, and when the work was completed, the master masons would migrate to other countries to construct other great works. My grandfather was a master mason, as was my father. I too became a master mason, both operative and speculative, and I traveled to distant lands to find work. Eventually, my work brought me to this great country, America, where my skills became well known and respected. William C.C. Claiborne Jr., President of the Jean Lafitte Historical Society in New Orleans, contacted me. The Historical Society was interested in restoring the blacksmith shop of the pirate Jean Lafitte, which is located on the corner of Bourbon Street and St. Phillip Street. It was built sometime before 1772, and had burnt down twice in the 1700s. The Historical Society wanted me to restore it to its original state. They told me they wanted to make it a tourist attraction. I was offered a fair price to do the work and a bonus if I completed it within the time allotted me, so I re-located to New Orleans to rebuild the shop. Mr. Claiborne came by on a daily basis to see how I was progressing. And because of his numerous visits, I felt as though he expected me to find something I'm sure he thought was hidden there. I'm not going to bore you with the details of the work I did, except to say that I started to rebuild the forge located in the center of the shop's main room, which was in a sad state of decay. Once I saw the condition of the forge, I knew I would have to find the plans and rebuild it to its exact specifications. So I began to take it apart so that I could rebuild it exactly the way it was originally designed for the Lafitte brothers. The bricks fell away into a heap whenever I pulled one down. Mr. Claiborne spent most of the day in that room watching me work. He studied every part of the material I removed from the room and was constantly looking over my shoulder, as if he were waiting for me to find something. He was becoming more of a nuisance than an asset and began to interfere with my work, so I spoke to him about it. He said he was interested in my progress and didn't realize he was interfering with my work. I didn't believe a word he said, and I was on my guard from that moment on, just in case there was something there to be found.

It was when I started to take apart the base of the forge that I found a hollow in the center of the forge that was covered with a metal sheet under a layer of bricks. I removed the sheet and found a secret compartment that held the box you now see before you and two large leather pouches containing precious jewels. There were also four additional leather pouches filled with gold coins. In this chest, you will find one of the bags of jewels and one bag of gold coins, as well as a Masonic codebook. I know that Dominique Youx, Lafitte's half-brother and a hero of the Battle of New Orleans, was a Mason and, although I could never prove it, I have reason to believe that Jean Lafitte and his brother Pierre were also Masons. It would explain why Lafitte wouldn't take the English offer of £30,000 in gold and a captaincy in their navy. A Freemason would never betray his country.

You will notice when you examine the Masonic codebook that Lafitte's name is written on the inside cover, so I must assume this was his very own codebook. You will also find a parchment written in Lafitte's own hand, telling of a great treasure hidden somewhere in New Orleans. The clues are all contained in the codebook and the parchment. While I was renovating the blacksmith shop, there were hard men with Mr. Claiborne, snooping around the shop, asking a lot of questions, obviously looking for what I had found. I think they were descendants of the men who sailed with Lafitte who knew of the treasure, but did not know where he had hidden it; but they may also have been the descendants of Governor Claiborne. I couldn't be sure. But I did make up my mind to tell you to contact Lafitte's heirs to possibly arrange with them to find the treasure together. I didn't trust the people I was working for and feared that if they discovered I actually found what they had been waiting centuries for that they would do me harm. I continued my work as if I had discovered nothing and I was very careful with the treasure I had found. I immediately covered the base permanently with bricks and mortar, making sure it appeared to be simply part of the renovation. I'm sure Claiborne was behind it when I discovered I was being watched and followed; and my hotel room appeared to have been searched a number of times. I had secreted the treasure in my toolbox and took a little out each day. When I went to the bank to cash my check, I transferred the contents of my toolbox to a safe deposit box, making sure my actions appeared part of the procedure of cashing my check. I cannot caution you enough. Be careful at all times, always suspect everyone, and trust no one, not even your closest friends. Just as I have given you my secrets, I'm sure our enemies have also given their secrets to their heirs. During the entire reconstruction of the shop, I was constantly being followed, so I could never take the time to attempt to find the larger treasure I'm sure exists, just as the treasure in the forge existed. I am sure you will be the one to find the larger treasure. When I finished my work ahead of schedule on the blacksmith shop, the Society gave me a bonus, telling me how happy they were with my work. I thanked them and, when I left, acted as if nothing out of the ordinary had happened. I left the treasure in the bank's safe deposit box for three years until I was sure those following me had given up. Then I quietly went in disguise to New Orleans to reclaim it. As soon as I returned to New York, I sold some of the jewels and gold coins. I went to a prestigious law firm, one that came highly recommended. The trust was set up the way I wanted, and now you know the rest.

"If I planned correctly, the trust fund should provide you with enough money for you to enjoy your life. The jewels and gold coins I left you will make you a rich man. I wanted to make sure you were mature enough to handle what I am giving you without changing you at your core. The larger treasure will make you famous. The treasure should be comparable to the treasure of Monte Cristo. Please do your best to seek out and find the descendants of Jean Lafitte and help them discover their true inheritance. It is the honorable thing to do.

I wish I could have seen you grow up. I would hope you are a Mason because all of the Calto men have been Masons. If you have to trust someone, don't trust them with everything.

Your loving great-great-grandfather,
Pietro Calto

Eddie sat back in his seat and thought about his ancestor's warning. "Trust no one, not even your friends." He was glad he didn't call Al and ask him for help. Al was probably all right, but now Eddie knew he couldn't trust anyone; he'd have to go it alone.

Chapter 6

Eddie decided to go down to the firehouse and have lunch with the guys. If they didn't know by now, he'd bring them up to date on what was happening with him and, after lunch, he'd clean out his locker. Just a few days had passed since the accident, and even though he was no longer a member of the company, it was great seeing the guys. He was amazed how much junk he had in his locker, the accumulation of twelve years of use.

When he went down the spiral staircase to the apparatus floor, he noticed a sentence written on the blackboard: "WHO WAS EDDIE CALTO?" Every time a man retired from this firehouse, that sentence was written on the blackboard with just the name changed. It was a tradition in this old firehouse and no one was excluded. Eddie smiled and went into the kitchen, where the guys were all kidding him over his retirement. They told him that lunch was lunch, but dinner was going to be something special. They had planned a farewell dinner for Eddie, at which he was to be the guest of honor. The real reason for the farewell dinner was the plaque he would receive from the company, commemorating his years on the job, with the date of his appointment and the date of his retirement etched on the brass plate screwed onto the walnut commemorative plaque. Eddie loved these guys. He realized that after 9-11, the experienced guys were leaving the job faster than anyone could have imagined. The senior man in the FDNY today averaged five years on the job. In the old days, he would still be a Johnny carrying the can (extinguisher).

Three months had passed and the injury to Eddie's knee healed perfectly, except for a little pain when he knelt. Other than that, he was in good shape. During his convalescence, he hired a private detective to locate an heir of Jean or Pierre Lafitte. A few days later, he received a phone call, and then a visit from Edward Gentile, the private detective he had hired.

"I have good news for you, Mr. Calto. I found a direct descendant of Pierre Lafitte, a Ms. Julianna Montaigne. Here's her home address and her telephone numbers, both work and cell."

Eddie thanked the man and paid him the agreed-upon price for four days' work. When Gentile left, Eddie picked up the phone and called Julianna Montaigne's cell phone. A pleasant feminine voice answered.

"This is Julianna."

"Ms. Montaigne, my name is Eddie Calto. You don't know me, but I've come into some private information concerning Jean Lafitte and a treasure he supposedly buried somewhere in New Orleans. I'd like to discuss this with you personally. I can either come to you or, if you can arrange it, you can visit me here in New York."

The million dollars from the trust fund made the transition to civilian life a lot easier for Eddie, but he wasn't about to tell any of his buddies about it. He made up his mind to take his ancestor's advice and not tell anyone about his inheritance or about the adventure on which he was about to embark. Eddie's mother had died of Hodgkin's disease when he was twenty-seven years old and had just joined the FDNY. He wished his father was still alive to help him find the treasure but, unfortunately, his father had died at a construction site in a scaffolding accident.

Eddie had hidden the parchment in a drainpipe in the

basement of his one-family house. Although Eddie never followed the trade of a master mason, he had learned his skills from his father, who was an expert in masonry. He had renovated his house when he first bought it, and while doing so had discovered a nook under the grating covering the drainpipe. He built a hidden compartment behind the bricks where the nook was situated. When he had finished his renovation, there was a large hole or compartment built into the nook, which he covered with false brick. Not even an expert could tell there was a hidden compartment there. He took the parchment and the teak box and placed it in the hidden receptacle.

Eddie wasn't taking any chances, so he had special locks put on his doors and windows. Then he had the finest alarm system money could buy installed throughout the house. He knew a good professional thief could circumvent just about any alarm, but he wasn't going to make it easy for them to walk into his house and rob him. Eddie checked to make sure the windows were locked tightly, then went down to the hidden compartment, retrieved the parchment, and placed it next to the Masonic codebook on the table. He took a yellow lined pad, like those secretaries use, from his desk and placed it on the table beside the parchment. He read the short note written on it.

my br, in o tt u ma btr undrstd wt is t fol, u ms fnd 29 n pl dr at the first st louis there you will find the widows son n eureka u ms rmv. jl.

Eddie, being a Mason, understood the first part of the code because it was written in basic Masonic code, which any Master Mason could decipher. The rest of the code baffled him. It didn't make any sense. He would have to study the words carefully. It had to be something very simple, something obvious; possibly a substitute word code or something just as simple. The sudden ringing of the doorbell jolted him from his thoughts. He placed everything in the cabinet above the sink and walked to the front door. When he opened the door, he thought he was dreaming. He became tongue-tied and unable to speak when he saw who was standing there. Eddie didn't get surprised often. Then again, he didn't often find a beautiful woman standing at the door waiting to be invited in. He smiled. "Can I help you?"

"Are you Mr. Calto?"

"Yes, I am. What can I do for you?"

"I'm Julianna Montaigne. We spoke on the phone a week ago and agreed we should meet. May I come in?"

"Please do. I just made a pot of coffee. Would you care for a cup?"

"Yes. Thank you. A cup of coffee sounds good."

He opened the door wider and she followed him into the kitchen. "Please have a seat. Be prepared for a cup of the finest coffee in town."

She smiled at Eddie.

"How do you take your coffee?"

"A little cream and one sugar please."

While the coffee was brewing, Eddie was curious. "Well, since you already know my name, what should I call you, Julianna? Julie?"

"Julianna," she said, putting out her hand for him to shake.

"I'm very pleased to meet you, Julianna."

As Eddie went to get the coffee, Julianna studied him carefully with a professional eye and liked what she saw. *I wonder if he's got a steady girl?*

Eddie poured two cups, sat opposite her and studied her face carefully. He got nothing from it other than that it was a very pretty face. Eventually, it was she who started the conversation.

"When you spoke to me on the phone last week, you said you had information that could possibly lead me to the treasure Lafitte supposedly buried in New Orleans in the early 1800s."

"Yes. One of my ancestors worked on the Lafitte blacksmith shop and found something. He didn't trust the Claiborne heir that kept hovering over him. He felt if he found something it didn't belong to anyone but a direct descendant of Lafitte. And that's why I called you."

She smiled and relaxed. "By any chance, could your ancestor's name happen to be Pietro Calto?"

"Why, yes. How did you know?"

"My mother and I discovered a diary in my grandfather's trunk and the diary mentioned a treasure that was hidden in Jean Lafitte's blacksmith shop in New Orleans. I immediately went to New Orleans and visited the blacksmith shop. I found that his shop had been renovated in 1928. I did some research and found that a Pietro Calto did the renovations. When I got back home, I was about to hire a detective to track down the heirs of this man, but before I could, you called me."

Eddie nodded thoughtfully. "Does anyone else know about this so-called treasure? Have you told anyone else about it or the diary?"

"No. I haven't told a soul. When you suggested we get together to compare notes, I came here directly from Saint Louis, Missouri."

"Before we go any further, prove to me that you are who you say you are."

She reached into her pocketbook, took out the diary she spoke of and handed it to him. She explained that Jean Lafitte's brother Pierre wrote the diary and it was discovered only recently in an old trunk stored in the attic of the family home.

Eddie inclined his head. He had made up his mind to share the jewels and gold coins with her, but not now. It wasn't the right time. He didn't want anything to interfere with them finding the treasure. He thought about telling her of the parchment, but remembered his great-great-grandfather's warning. On the other hand, if there was a treasure and it was as large as his great-great-grandfather said it was, she had as much right to it as he did. He had no qualms about sharing it.

Eddie held the diary, but he wanted more, so he asked to see her driver's license and voter's registration card. He wanted to copy them on his Epson printer. "Please don't get offended, but I want to know who I'm dealing with before we continue this conversation." When he came back into the kitchen, she looked at him with a hopeful, expectant look on her face. "Tell me about yourself," Eddie said. He wanted to know all he could about her before he went against his great-great-grandfather's wishes and committed himself to this beautiful woman who could, in fact, be the enemy.

She explained that she lived in St. Louis, Missouri and had graduated recently from college. She then took a job as a nurse with a local hospital.

"Are you working now?" he asked.

"I took a leave of absence in case I needed more time to search for the treasure. I just hope that when I return, I have a job to go back to."

Eddie dismissed the notion with a wave of his hand. "Don't worry about a job. When you return home, you're gonna have a ton of money, so don't worry your pretty little head over your job. Let's concentrate on finding the treasure."

"You seem so sure there is a treasure."

"I know there's a treasure, and we're going to find it."

"What if there is no treasure and you waste all your time and money chasing a dream?"

"There's a treasure; I just know it. I can feel it."

"I agree. I feel the same way." She became animated as she talked and Eddie couldn't help but enjoy listening to her. He liked this girl and felt comfortable working with her. Then the thought occurred to him that maybe she was married, or engaged; or maybe she had a boyfriend.

"Won't your husband miss you while you're gone?"

"Oh no. I'm not married."

"Well, what about your boyfriend? Surely someone as attractive as you must have a boyfriend at home, waiting for you?"

"No, I have no one. I guess I've been too busy with my career to find the time for a relationship."

"Before I discuss my plans with you, you must promise you will not repeat or discuss anything I'm about to tell you with anyone, under any circumstance. Is that understood?"

"Yes."

"And do you agree to my conditions?"

"Yes."

"Do you have the time it will take to see this adventure through to its end?"

"Yes."

"Where are you staying?"

"At a Days Inn, not far from here."

"You have to check out of there and stay here with me. I'll drive you to pick up your bags. I have an extra room with a separate bath and your room has a lock on it. I'm not making a pass at you; it's just that I was warned not to trust anyone and not to say anything to anyone. So I'm going out on a limb; and if I'm going to do this against my better judgment, I would like you here where I can keep an eye on you until I get to know you better. And please don't be offended; it's nothing personal. When you are comfortably settled into your room,

I'll explain everything I know, and maybe together we can sort it out."

She smiled sweetly at him. "As long as there is a lock on the door and I have the key, I see no problem moving into your spare room, Eddie."

Before Eddie left the house, he remembered seeing a movie in which whenever a man left his home he pulled a hair from his head, wet it with his saliva, and placed it by the door. If someone entered the house, he would know by the hair either being there or not. It was a simple precaution, and that's what he decided to do. Julianna watched, then they left to get his car, parked in the garage behind his house.

Before driving Julianna to her hotel, Eddie took side streets, back tracked, and went around the block a few times just in case they were being followed. He parked in front of her hotel and waited while she went inside to pick up her luggage.

While Julianna checked out, Eddie took her luggage and put it in the trunk of the car. On the drive back to his house, Eddie informed her that they were first going to stop for a bite to eat in a very special restaurant, and he wasn't taking no for an answer. "We can talk over drinks, and then, when we're ready, we'll order our food." She liked a man who took charge and since she hadn't eaten all day she agreed.

They went to Raphaela's Italian Restaurant. It was a neighborhood restaurant with great Italian food. He pulled into the parking lot and gave his key to the parking lot attendant. When they entered the restaurant, Richie the headwaiter greeted them. Richie wasn't a neighborhood guy, but Eddie had a lot of respect for him because he raised his two kids all by himself when his wife left him and the babies for a dancer. Through the years, Eddie had become a frequent visitor at Raphaela's. He and Richie got to know one another well and, as time passed, they became close friends. Eddie introduced

Julianna to him and Richie greeted her with all the charm that a headwaiter and sometime bartender could muster up, which is generous, to say the least. With a nod of his head, he motioned towards a waiter and, before the waiter arrived, Richie informed Eddie that he would stop by their table later. The waiter led the handsome couple to a cozy table by the window with an unromantic view of Roosevelt Avenue. Eddie ordered a rum and Coke and explained to Julianna, "I'm not a big drinker, so if I'm only going to have one or two drinks, I'll order rum and Coke or a gin and tonic. If I'm with friends and plan on doing some serious drinking—which is rare—I drink scotch and water."

They sat and chatted over their drinks and, as the minutes ticked by, became comfortable with each other. They sipped their drinks slowly, enjoying each other's company and hoping the time would pass slowly until they were ready to order their meal. The chemistry between them was wonderful and they chatted as easily as if they had known each other for years. Julianna asked Eddie what he recommended and he suggested, "Pasta, if you like pasta. Then, anything you order here will be delicious. The food is cooked by Grandma Raphaela herself and she's from the old country, so she will not serve anything in her restaurant that she would not eat at home. And do you see those two men in tuxedos?"

"Yes."

"They're her sons and they make sure the food you get is cooked to perfection."

"Do they make a good eggplant parmesan? I had it once when I came to New York on vacation with my mother."

"They make the best eggplant parmesan. Try it, and if you don't like it, I'll order something else for you. Deal?"

"Deal."

Eddie ordered eggplant parmesan for Julianna and tilapia

francese for himself. He followed this with expensive bottles of red wine for himself and white for Julianna, which Richie picked for them. Now that Eddie had money, he could afford to do what he always wanted to do, and that was not worry about the bill which, in this case, would be rather high. Talk about luck; a few months ago, Eddie could never have afforded to have dinner with a beautiful woman in an expensive place like this. But tonight was a different story. He was rich now, and it couldn't have come at a better time.

Richie, although he was the head waiter, had a specialty that he saved for special customers. He rolled a cart with a large bowl and various ingredients and parked it beside their table. Then he began a ceremony that, when completed, would result in a fantastic Caesar salad. He made it all by hand, using his fork to mash the anchovies and, when it was finished, Julianna confessed that she had never tasted a Caesar salad as pleasurable or tasty as this one. Richie beamed with pride when she said that and told her he would be back in a little while with a copy of his special recipe. They were having such a good time that they never got around to discussing the treasure.

"Have you ever had an Italian cannoli for desert?" asked Eddie.

"No."

So he ordered one for each of them with a cup of espresso for him and a cappuccino for her.

"How could anyone in this beautiful country not have tasted a cannoli, especially you, who appear to appreciate the finer things in life?"

She looked a little embarrassed. "I guess I've been too busy studying and not taking the time to socialize. But this cannoli is delicious." Then she added, "But I'll never go to dinner with you again."

Eddie almost panicked. He wanted to have many other

dinners with her like this one. "Why won't you go to dinner with me?"

Julianna laughed . "If I had dinner with you every night and ate the way I did tonight, I'd weigh 300 pounds in no time at all."

"Whew, you had me worried there for a minute."

She laughed and he wanted to laugh with her because she captivated him.

Chapter 7

The man in the black Mercedes was a professional thief who had no problem finding where Eddie Calto lived. He parked the car opposite Eddie's house on the other side of the school on 41st Avenue, where Calto wouldn't see his car if he happened to be looking in that direction when he stepped out of his house. The man wore sunglasses, a Mets jacket, and baseball cap and he stood waiting at the entrance of the empty schoolyard with a paper in his hand, facing Eddie's house. He leaned casually against the fence. Just a man reading a newspaper; only he wasn't reading it, he was looking over it. He was a patient man who knew that sooner or later Eddie would have to leave his home. When he did, he would break in and perform a thorough search, which he knew from experience always brought favorable results. He had broken into hundreds of homes and he always found what he was looking for, no matter how well it was hidden.

The front door opened and Calto stepped out, accompanied by a beautiful woman, and it appeared that they might be going to dinner. Normally, the man would have followed them, but his orders were to secure the box. He waited for them to drive away, then folded the newspaper and walked back to his black Mercedes, where he threw the newspaper on the front seat, opened the glove compartment, and took out a small leather bag, which he put in the side pocket of his jacket. He locked the doors to the Mercedes, then walked across the schoolyard to Eddie's house. He had no idea what was in the box that his client wanted, but that was none of his concern. He was getting paid handsomely to find the box and take it to his employer.

The man did his best not to look conspicuous and he was successful to a point, but he couldn't help his appearance. He was of average height, but rail thin with a sinister pockmarked face and dead eyes sunk into hollow sockets. He was a frightening looking man who had a face that was hard to forget. Having performed this type of entry many times before, he stood outside the door, studying it carefully, looking for any telltale sign of a trap. From experience, he could tell there was none. Not knowing what type of alarm he would have to neutralize, he walked around the house and headed down the alley until he stopped by a window. He could see the magnets placed strategically on the window and thought he recognized the type of alarm Calto had installed. He couldn't be certain, of course, until he got inside, and then he'd only have fifteen seconds in which to silence the alarm, or else he'd be forced to leave in a hurry. He felt certain he could overcome this alarm, having neutralized just about every type of alarm imaginable. No, it wasn't the alarm that worried him; it was the fifteen seconds he had to shut it off. It wouldn't be hard to do if he knew where the main box was located. Most alarms were placed in the hallway between the main part of the house and the bedroom. He looked around to see if anyone was near. It wouldn't pay to be caught by a nosy neighbor, looking into someone's home like a Peeping Tom. He looked over his shoulder at the neighboring houses' windows. Satisfied there was no threat there, he stretched himself up to the window and took a quick look into the room, trying to spot the alarm. This window only showed him the kitchen area. Maybe the window further down the alley might give him a better view. He walked quietly down to the next window and looked around once again, knowing that this was the point when he was the most vulnerable. He had to do this fast before someone spotted him, so he pulled himself up as high as he could and looked inside . . . and there it was, right where he thought it would be. He laughed to himself as he walked back to the front of the house. Those installers are so predictable, placing the main box where it's easiest for them to install, rather than hiding it where it would do the customer the most good. Now that he knew where the alarm was located, he'd have no problem breaking in and shutting the alarm off within fifteen seconds. He walked around to the front door and was inside the house within seconds. He raced over to the master alarm, took the leather bag from his side pocket, and pulled out a set of special burglar picks. The seconds ticked by as he hurriedly selected the proper picks and used them to open the box, and then hastily neutralized the alarm. He thought he might have gone over the fifteen-second limit, but sometimes the installer set the timer for up to a minute before the alarm would trigger. He just hoped a secondary silent alarm wasn't installed. Well, he couldn't worry about that now; he had to go through the house and do a thorough search.

Most people kept a safe in their bedrooms and Eddie was no different. He used this safe, installed by the previous owner, for keeping his passport, deed, and miscellaneous papers; nothing really of any importance. The man spotted the safe immediately. He was the best at locating safes that were hidden from view. He used a high tech electronic keyboard and had the safe opened in seconds. This wasn't even a challenge for him, but he was disappointed to see that there was no teak box. He wondered if this safe was even big enough to hold the box. Being a professional, he closed the safe and looked around the room to make sure he hadn't disturbed anything else. Satisfied that nothing was amiss, he quickly searched the other rooms. Nothing. The box must be hidden downstairs, he thought.

He raced down the stairs into the cellar and studied it

carefully, using his years of experience in finding elusive hiding places. He'd find this hiding place if there was one to be found. After checking every inch of the cellar and finding nothing, there was only one other place it could be and that was in the drain. He lifted the grating, took his flash light out, and scanned the surrounding walls. He couldn't see anything remotely suspicious, so he banged the surrounding walls of the drainage pit with his flashlight, hoping to hear a hollow sound. There was none. Eddie had replaced the brick just for that reason. If anyone tried to hit it to find the hollow spot, it wouldn't work because the bricks were secured to a metal swivel that, when it was locked in place, became a permanent part of the drain wall.

The man looked at his watch. Time to go. He'd been here longer than he intended. He'd have to return another time to continue his search. He knew there must be another safe hidden somewhere in this house and, being the professional he was, he didn't want a one-time failure to blemish his sterling record. No, he was convinced there was a second safe hidden in this house somewhere, but where? He'd read Calto's record that Claiborne had handed him. The guy was just a fireman who knew nothing about security. Calto must have called in a company to install the alarm, and the alarm was a good one, but it was child's play to this man. He looked around the cellar once again, just to make sure he hadn't missed anything, then shook his head and bounded up the stairs as silent as a cat. Well, it's not down there, he said to himself. That would make it easier for him the next time, because now he could eliminate the cellar and concentrate on the upper part of the house. Maybe it was in the crawl space in the attic. He hadn't checked there because of the time constraints, but next time that would be the first place he would look.

Chapter 8

While driving back to his house after dinner, Eddie drove around the block once as a precaution to see if there were any unfamiliar cars parked near or around his house. Having lived in this neighborhood for years, he knew most of the neighborhood cars, and he didn't see any unusual vehicles parked near his home. So he pulled in front of his house and parked by the curb. When he approached his front door, he looked for the strand of hair he had placed on the door—and it was gone! Someone had been here, he was sure of it. He left Julianna in the kitchen and raced down the stairs and into the cellar, where he checked his special hiding place. He was relieved to find the burglar hadn't discovered it. He didn't think his hidden safe would be found, but when a professional thief breaks into your home, you can never be sure.

After checking everything, Eddie made a pot of Italian espresso and set it down on the end table beside a bottle of Sambuca.

"Have you ever tasted Italian Espresso with Sambuca?"

"No" she replied. "I never tasted either."

"Well, then, you're in for a treat." He poured three-fourths of a cup of espresso into each cup and then he poured the Sambuca reverently, filling the cup to the brim. Sambuca is a licorice-flavored liquor favored by the Italians and is similar to anisette. But Sambuca is much stronger—and to Eddie it was much more enjoyable, especially when taken with espresso. Some of the older Italian men liked to dip the tip of the unlit end of their cigars in the Sambuca while having their demitasse. The flavor of the Sambuca mixed with the smoke gave a new meaning to the pleasure of smoking a cigar. "How do you like it?" he asked.

"Different," she replied.

"I should have started you with a half a shot of the drink and then added more until you had the exact taste you preferred." But he needn't have worried about whether the drink was too strong, because when he offered her another cup, she took it without hesitating.

"How did you enjoy your first cup of Italian coffee?" he asked after they had finished.

"It was surprisingly good. I didn't think I would like it, but I did."

Eddie was glad. This seemed genuine coming from her and not something she would say just to make him feel good.

With that out of the way, he suggested a partnership between them, but a knock on the door made them both jump. Eddie cautiously looked out the peephole and was relieved to see his friend, Frank Scaffo, a firefighter from his company.

"Frankie, what are you doing here?"

"You forgot this." He handed Eddie a small box.

"Thanks for bringing this to me. I hadn't realized I left it in my locker."

"Yeah, your replacement found it on the upper shelf and brought it to the captain who put it in a drawer and almost forgot about it. Since I don't live too far from you he gave it to me and told me to tell you he's sorry he didn't get it to you sooner."

Eddie took it and invited Frankie in. "Frank, meet Julianna. Julianna, this is my friend, Frankie. We worked together."

Julianna shook Frankie's hand. "Pleased to meet you." She looked at the box and her curiosity got the best of her. "What's in the box?"

Eddie's face reddened. "Nothing really. Just a memento

from the job."

"Yeah, some memento," Frankie said, laughing.

"Yeah, well, let's not go into that now."

Frankie took the hint and, seeing the coffee cups and the Sambuca on the table, poured himself a cup of coffee. Then he turned to Julianna. "So, when did you two meet?"

"Actually we met today, and we were just discussing a distant relative of hers, Pierre Lafitte."

"He was the famous pirate, right?"

"No that was his brother, Jean."

"Why were you discussing him?"

Eddie wanted to change the subject but Julianna answered the question for him. "I found his brother Pierre's diary and Eddie suggested I should have it appraised to see what it's worth. That's what we were discussing when you knocked on the door."

That satisfied Frankie and they sat back and chatted over coffee for a little while longer, until Frankie looked at his watch. "Wow, I didn't realize I'd been here this long. I gotta go, but keep in touch, okay?"

"Will do, Frankie."

"Nice meeting you, Julianna."

"Yes. The same here." While Eddie walked Frankie to the door, Julianna picked up the box and opened it. She was surprised to find a medal for bravery issued by the New York City Fire Department. She quickly closed the box and replaced it where it was.

Now that Frankie had left, they continued their discussion. But it was Eddie who spoke first.

"Look, my ancestor left instructions for me to contact a Lafitte heir and since you are that person and you didn't come empty handed, I have a proposition for you. And if you agree, we would share whatever treasure we find. That is, if there is any treasure."

She thought for a minute. It was true that she was the legitimate heir to Lafitte's treasure, but Eddie held the clues, and she felt more comfortable searching for the treasure with a man. So she agreed to share the treasure equally with him, and they shook hands on it.

Since they were now partners, Eddie decided he would share the jewels and gold coins Pietro Calto had left for him with her as well, but not right at this moment. First, he took out the parchment and showed it to her.

my br, in o tt u ma btr undrstd wt is t fol, u ms fnd 29 n pl dr at the first st louis there you will find the widows son n eureka u ms rmv. jl

Julianna read the words carefully, then looked up at him and shook her head. "I can't make heads or tails out of this. Can you interpret it?"

Eddie nodded and explained it to her. "The first part is a simple Masonic code that I can interpret. Here, let me read it to you. 'My brother, in order that you may better understand what is to follow, you must find 29 in pl dr...' I don't know what he means by 'pl dr,' but I'm sure it has a simple solution. Lafitte would have wanted to confuse a layman, but not a fellow Mason. I just have to think about where he's leading us."

After a moment, Eddie looked up suddenly. "Come with me."

"Where are we going?"

"To my study. I want to check out some of my other Masonic books."

"You're a Freemason too?"

"Yep. All the men in my family were Freemasons. I don't go to lodge as often as I would like to, but I keep my dues current and someday I'd like to go through the chairs."

"What does that mean, going through the chairs?"

"It means someday I'd like to become master of the lodge, but in order to do that, I'd have to work myself up through the various positions or chairs. Do you know that George Washington took his oath of office on a Masonic bible dressed in full Masonic raiment? And many of the signers of the Declaration of Independence, such as Benjamin Franklin and John Hancock, were Masons?"

"No, I didn't."

"Did you ever hear of the poem by Longfellow? 'Listen my children, and you shall hear of the midnight ride of Paul Revere'? Even Paul Revere, a member of St. Andrews's Lodge, interrupted his duties as Senior Deacon at the Green Dragon Tavern to go on his midnight run. The Boston tea party was a Masonic act and the US Constitution is a Masonic document."

"Wow, I didn't know any of this."

Eddie scanned the shelves as he talked, looking for any book that might give him a clue to what "pl dr" could represent. Buried on the upper shelf, in the right hand corner, were two small books that were almost hidden. He reached up, took them down, and realized he might have hit pay dirt. The first book was the small blue-jacketed New York Masonic codebook, but the second book was the one he needed. *Duncan's Ritual of Freemasonry*. *Duncan's Ritual* wasn't written until 1976, but it contained important Masonic information, so he took that book and the blue codebook into the kitchen and they again read the code on the parchment.

my br, in o tt u ma btr undrstd wt is t fol, u ms fnd 29 n pl dr at the first st louis there you will find the widows son n eureca u ms rmv. jl

"It appears the parchment is telling us to go to St Louis first, but that would be heading west, not east." Was "29" an address? He knew who the widow's son was, but how would he find him in St. Louis?

Julianna quietly said, "You said Lafitte would have kept his code simple. Maybe you're looking too deeply into it."

Eddie realized she was right. He went to his computer and did a search for "First Saint Louis." The hits he found were irrelevant, so he tried again. He typed: "First St. Louis." This produced far too many results to be useful. Next he typed "First St. Louis in New Orleans." Bingo! He got a ton of useful hits. One of these was the St. Louis Cathedral, New Orleans. Another was St. Louis Cathedral, Jackson Square, New Orleans, Louisiana. But the most promising links were for St. Louis Cemetery. So he decided to do another search using "First St. Louis Cemetery in New Orleans." He hit the jackpot when he found a glossary of famous persons buried at the First St. Louis Cemetery. However, there wasn't any mention of a Lafitte.

One of the links had a phone number as well as an address, so Eddie called the number and a gentleman answered the phone. Eddie casually mentioned that he was thinking of taking a trip to New Orleans and that he'd like to visit the First St. Louis Cemetery. He was particularly interested to know if Jean Lafitte was buried there.

"No, he's not buried here."

Eddie sighed and the person on the other end of the phone, hearing his disappointment, tried to placate him. "But his brother Pierre is buried here as well as Dominique Youx and many of the men that fought with Lafitte."

"Well, that settles it then. We'll come to New Orleans and make a special trip to your cemetery . . . and the First St. Louis Cemetery has you to thank for us making the trip. I want to thank you for your time and your professionalism."

The man thanked Eddie profusely and told him his name was Pierre. If they had any other questions they should call him. Eddie said he would, and thanked him once again.

"Okay, that helps a lot. Let's take another look at what's left of the code."

my br, in o tt u ma btr undrstd wt is t fol, u ms rd 29 n pl dr at the first st louis there you will find the widows son n eureca u ms rmv. jl

"Twenty-nine could be an address but, then again, maybe not. Let's assume it's the cemetery. As for the widow's son, I will know him when I find him. Pack your bags; we're leaving for New Orleans."

Chapter 9

Even though it was evening, Eddie called a private security firm and, without questioning their fee, he hired them to watch his home while he was gone, with instructions not to call him while he was away, but to handle the situation as they saw fit. The manager assured Eddie that one of their operatives would be at his home early the following morning to meet him before he left.

At 5:30 the following morning, after meeting the security agency's operative, Eddie took Julianna for breakfast. They parked in long-term parking at JFK and boarded the 7:30 a.m. non-stop flight to New Orleans. The plane landed at Louis Armstrong New Orleans International Airport at 11:05 a.m. After retrieving their luggage, they took a cab to the five-star Le Pavilion hotel. Eddie had money now, and while he was in New Orleans he wanted to live large. Eddie chose this hotel because, according to the brochure he picked up at the airport, it had a stunning lobby with high ceilings, grand columns, Oriental rugs, detailed woodwork, and eleven crystal chandeliers. The brochure described the tasteful, luxurious guest rooms decorated with original artwork and antiques, proudly announcing that it was built in 1907 and was the first hotel in New Orleans with elevators installed. It even had a heated pool on the roof. But the real reason Eddie liked it was because it was conveniently close to all major New Orleans attractions. This hotel was exactly where he wanted to stay.

"How do you like the hotel?" Eddie asked.

"I'm impressed with it. I love the opulence of the lobby, but can we afford it?"

Eddie tried but failed to suppress a smile. "You can't, but I can. My great-great-grandfather recently left me a trust fund with over a million dollars in it and I was looking for a good excuse to spend some of the money. This looks like as good a place as any to start."

Julianna raised an eyebrow when Eddie mentioned the million dollar trust fund. "Now I don't feel bad spending some of your money," she said smiling. They walked to the desk to check in and Eddie told the clerk he wanted one of the best rooms the hotel had to offer. He asked him to describe the better suites.

The desk clerk explained that the most expensive suite was the Presidential, which offered a library, dining room, and two bedrooms with private baths. What turned Eddie off about the Presidential suite was that each bedroom had two king-sized beds, which he didn't need, so he ruled that one out. The other two suites were the New Orleans, which had a plantation theme with antiques by famous New Orleans craftsmen, many of which came from local homes. The suite had four-poster beds in two bedrooms, each with a foyer and parlor. A former slave by the name of C. Lee built one of the beds circa 1855. The suite also sported the original chandelier from 1907 in the suite's parlor. Eddie didn't care for this suite either. The clerk explained that Suite 330 was superb and was his favorite. It had a contemporary theme, which incorporated a touch of French Empire styling, including private baths, a spacious parlor, virtual fireplace, and a wet bar. Just what the doctor ordered. Eddie wanted Julianna in the same suite with him and he wanted her to be comfortable, but he didn't want her to think he was hitting on her, so he chose Suite 330 because of the privacy. It wasn't as large as the others, but to Eddie it was cozy and more comfortable.

After paying for the suite, they took the elevator to the third floor, then walked the short distance to their suite. Eddie was pleasantly surprised by the romantic ambience and the sumptuous splendor of their rooms. He'd obviously chosen the right suite, and he paused for a moment to reassess its exorbitant cost. It looked to him like money well spent. The bellboy put their bags in their rooms and after Eddie tipped him, he mixed himself a rum and Coke, while Julianna freshened up. Then they went downstairs and shared enjoyable small talk over a leisurely lunch in the hotel restaurant.

Eddie was glad that Julianna had agreed to tag along on this adventure because he enjoyed her company more than he cared to admit. The way she smiled, the way she moved, the way she talked, and the way she pronounced her words. He loved all of it. She was a cool lady with no hidden agenda. What you saw was what you got and it was refreshing.

What bothered Eddie about the women he usually went out with was that they were constantly changing the rules whenever it suited them, but they never informed him of it. To paraphrase Frank Sinatra, when someone once asked him if he liked women, "I love them...I just don't understand them." Eddie thought of a divorced friend of his with two kids who met a woman. They became an item and fell in love. She wanted to get married, but his friend told her that if he were to get married, he didn't want any more children. She agreed and said she felt the same way; she didn't want any children either. So they got married. They were married six months when, one evening, out of nowhere, she said. "You know, I've been thinking about having kids."

He put up his hand and stopped her. "Don't go there," he said. "We both agreed we weren't having any kids."

She batted her eyelashes and purred coquettishly. "I know we agreed on it, but I changed my mind about having a baby, and I'd like to have one now."

She changed the rules without telling him and the marriage

failed. Julianna wasn't like that. She was different. But then, Eddie thought to himself, I'm not going out with her and I don't really know her, do I?

When they finished lunch, they walked through the hotel's air-conditioned lobby and out the front entrance into the fiery, hot, midday New Orleans summer heat, and into a waiting air-conditioned cab that took them directly to St. Louis Cemetery Number 1.

At the cemetery they joined a group of tourists, and followed along listening to their tour guide, a very knowledgeable and interesting older man who spoke with a Cajun accent. He told the group his name was Chubby, that he was eighty-one years old, and that he had buried people for fifty-one years. As they walked along the promenade, he pointed to the outer wall that he called "the wall of death," which was one city block long and, at one time, was five tiers high.

There were many important people buried in this cemetery in interesting tombs. Jean Etienne Bore, a wealthy pioneer of the sugar industry and the first mayor of New Orleans; Homer Plessy, the plaintiff from the landmark 1896 *Plessy v. Ferguson* Supreme Court decision on civil rights; Benjamin Latrobe, America's first professional architect; Ernest N. "Dutch" Morial, the first African-American mayor of New Orleans; Paul Morphy, one of the earliest world champions of chess, who would play four or five people at chess while blindfolded; and Marie Laveau, the legendary voodoo priestess, whose unmarked grave in the Glapion family crypt is perpetually decorated with gifts and marked with x's or crosses left by visitors. Eddie was particularly captivated by Marie Laveau, who Chubby described as the Queen of New Orleans; Chubby told the group she was buried there on June 11, 1897. Eddie noticed the letters XLT scratched onto the tomb and asked Chubby about it.

Chubby said it meant "Extra Luck and True." He explained the *gris gris* ritual to the group. "*Gris gris* drop the left foot on the *gris gris*, shuffle along pick it up the *gris gris*, stomp, pick up a piece of *gris gris* with your left hand and knock three times with your right hand then ask her for a favor, but don't tell anyone what the favor is or she will not grant it. Her last words, spoken three minutes before she died, were, 'Please remember me. I've been a good mother and a good friend. Please by passing here, pray for me. I regret anything wrong that I did, but I will do anything in my power to grant you. People all over the world come to New Orleans and knock three times and it shall be given to you.' The public says that the power was given to Marie Laveau and she died with it. She didn't leave it to no one or give it to no one. Therefore, she has a right to grant you that favor, but you can't tell anyone what the favor is or it won't be granted."

Chubby explained the custom behind the family vaults. When a person was buried, no formaldehyde was used to preserve the body if the family intended to re-use the tomb. No preservatives, or the tomb couldn't be re-used. Once a year, the caretaker pulled the casket out of the tomb then crawled about twelve feet into the crypt. The bones were picked up and placed in a metal box at the end of the crypt. The box contained a fluid that would dissolve the bones. The body only lasted one year and the tomb couldn't be opened but once a year. If a second family member died within the year, the family had to rent a tomb for storage until the year was up and the body could be transferred into its proper tomb. If you didn't have a tomb, you could rent one for a few hundred dollars a year, but no name could be put on the tomb because it was not your property.

They soon broke away from Chubby and the group. While they walked along the aisle of the dead, Eddie kept his eye out for any clue that might present itself to him. As he passed the many tombstones he searched every one, letting nothing escape his gaze. He noticed a young schoolteacher on a field trip, with students surrounding her, watching her with young inquisitive faces as she rubbed charcoal over a very thin sheet of paper. She had placed the paper, which was larger than the tombstone, over the front of the tombstone and secured it with masking tape. Then she carefully pulled the paper tightly against the stone and rubbed the front of the paper with charcoal to make an imprint on the paper of the tombstone's lettering. The end result was an exact imprint of the wording on the tomb, which would be used as part of the project she intended to use in her class. While rubbing the paper, she explained to the class in detail what she was doing and why. Then, satisfied that her rubbing had been successfully accomplished, she removed the paper.

It was only then that Eddie noticed the name on the tombstone. It was the tomb of Dominique Youx, the hero of the Battle of New Orleans and, more importantly, the half brother of Jean Lafitte. Eddie wasn't superstitious, but he felt that this was an auspicious sign. Here he was, looking for Jean Lafitte's treasure, and the first tomb they stopped to look at without a tour guide was that of Dominique Youx.

Having separated from the tour group, they kept walking in a different direction. Eddie was looking for a tomb with a particular name, a name that could hold the key to finding the treasure. As they wandered along the dirt walkway, they noticed the differences between the tombs. Some were well kept, but others had sunk into the ground. The strange part was that the tomb right next to a sunken tomb could remain upright and aboveground. One tomb sank and the one next to it didn't. Go figure. New Orleans is the only city in the USA that is beneath sea level, and bodies have to be buried above ground because of the water table. In the old days, when they buried bodies under the ground, sometimes after a heavy rain coffins as well as bodies would bubble to the surface. Eddie shook himself from his thoughts and took the copy of the parchment code from his pocket and re-read it.

my br, in o tt u ma btr undrstd wt is t fol, u ms fnd 29 n pl dr at the first st louis there you will find the widows son n eureca u ms rmv. jl

"Wait a minute. I think I know what 'pl dr' means. Hand me Pierre Laffite's diary. Julianna reached into her pocket book for the diary and handed it to him. "I think 'pl' is Pierre Lafitte's initials and 'dr' means diary. That must be it. 'Pl dr' has to mean Pierre Lafitte's diary. There's only one way to find out. Let's turn to page 29 and see what he wrote there. I was right. He's left us a clue."

n t es there you will find the widow's son.

"In the east, there, you will find the widow's son," Eddie translated. "The clue tells us that we should look to the east."

He took out a small compass and checked to see where east was, and then they headed in that direction. They walked down the easternmost row of tombstones and, when they reached the end, turned right onto the next aisle. They traveled about a third of the way down the aisle when Eddie spotted what he was looking for. The name on the tomb was Hiram Forsk and it had the prominent Freemason symbol of the square and compass above his name.

"Why did we stop at this tomb?"

"We've just found the tomb of the widow's son."

"How do you know this is the widow's son's tomb?"

"Because Hiram, the name on the tomb, is the name of the

widow's son. In Masonic legend, three ruffians tried to extort the secrets of Freemasonry from our Grand Master, Hiram Abiff, and when he wouldn't tell, they murdered him. The murder of our Grand Master was discovered and the ruffians were captured, tried, and put to death. No, this is the tomb Lafitte was pointing us to. Now we have to discover the clue he left behind for us." Eddie scoured the tomb, walking around it and checking all sides, but he couldn't find anything that would indicate it was hiding a clue. It must be something else, something simple. He studied the letters 'pthgr' and thought it could be a code for Pythagoras, so he took the copy of *Duncan's Ritual* from the side pocket of his jacket and looked for a reference to that name. The answer was on page 129.

"Pythagoras was a brother Mason who travelled through Asia, Africa, and Europe," Eddie read. "This wise philosopher enriched his mind abundantly in a general knowledge of things, and, more especially, in geometry or masonry." According to *Duncan's Ritual*, "He drew many problems and theorems and, among the most distinguished, he erected this, which in the joy of his heart he called Eureka, in the Grecian language signifying 'I have found it.'" The page had a design above the paragraph, explaining what "Eureka" meant. This time, Eddie looked at the tomb differently, knowing what he was looking for. He slowly examined the front of the tomb from top to bottom, then moved to the right side and looked for the sign, but didn't find it. He did the same with the other two sides and still found nothing. Could he be wrong? Could it be that there was no clue on this tomb? He didn't think so. He looked at the front of the tomb once again. Something caught his eye at the upper top left front. Eddie thought he noticed a brick with a faint design, barely noticeable, that looked as though it could have been worn down by the weather. It was situated near the top, a good place for it, he thought.

Eddie searched the ground for something like a nail to scratch away debris from the design or symbol. Something was hidden there behind the dirt and grime and he intended to find out what it was. He looked around, hoping no one was in the vicinity, but a few tourists were slowly making their way down the avenue of tombs. They would stop a minute to read an inscription on a tomb, then continue their leisurely walk. While Eddie waited for the tourists to pass, he spotted an empty vase that had once held flowers two tombs down. Although the flowers were gone, the vase still held water—probably collected from rain. He picked up the vase and took it to the tomb. When the small group of tourists had passed them, he splashed water on the face of the brick and the Pythagorean Eureka design jumped out at them. Eddie quickly read the code once again, looking for the next clue. The last few words told him all he needed to know: **u ms rmv**! "You Must Remove."

Chapter 10

The man with the pockmarked face, wearing the baseball cap, parked the black Mercedes around the corner where it couldn't be seen by his quarry. He sat in his car for ten minutes. Any longer and he felt he would arouse the curiosity of the neighbors. So he took his newspaper, walked to the corner deli, bought a cup of coffee, and walked down to the park, where he sat on a bench, purportedly to read his newspaper. The bench he had chosen had a direct view of the Calto house. He didn't know that Eddie Calto was in New Orleans and would not be returning for a while but, after a day and a half of surveillance, he decided it was time to re-visit the house. He took his lock pick and cupped it in his hand so it wouldn't be seen by someone walking past or by a nosy neighbor. He waited for the right moment. A moment when no one was close enough to see what he was about to do. He had the door opened and was in the house in a matter of seconds. But, to his surprise, he came face to face with a rather large man who was apparently as surprised as he was. The intruder reached for his gun, which was hidden under his jacket in a belt holster.

The security guard, whose instructions were to remain in the house until relieved by the next man, leaped at the intruder just as his gun cleared its holster. It went off as the two men grappled for control, hitting the light above the kitchen table. The guard had to neutralize the intruder's gun, making it a man-to-man fight, maybe to the death. The intruder was lighter and smaller than the agent, but he was wiry and knew how to handle himself. Another gunshot and the detective felt something punch into his side. But he held onto the gun

74

desperately, struggling to turn it towards the perpetrator. The guard's strength waned from loss of blood, but the smaller man was also weaker, having used all his strength trying to subdue the bigger man. And, ever so slowly, the intruder's arm turned towards him . . . and bang . . . another gunshot. This time it was the intruder who staggered backwards against the refrigerator, staring in disbelief at his stomach. As the blood pumped out in an increasingly wider circle, dampening his shirt, he fell to his knees. *This can't be happening to me.* With this final thought, his vision became blurry. The guard seemed to be pointing his gun at him, but he couldn't be sure. The burglar stayed in that position for a moment longer until the blurriness faded to black and he descended into death.

The security guard, weak from loss of blood, tied a towel tightly around his waist to staunch the blood flow to just a trickle, then called his office and told them he'd been shot and needed medical attention. They immediately called an ambulance and alerted the police, who responded to the address.

The paramedics cleaned the wound and gave the guard the good news. "The bullet passed right through your side from front to back without hitting a vital organ. You were very lucky, my friend."

Before the paramedics could take him to the ambulance and give him a blood transfusion, the police still had a few questions to ask.

"What's your name and what were you doing here?"

"I'm a security guard assigned to watch the premises because of a break in a few days ago."

"A break in? How come the police weren't called?"

"Because nothing was stolen. The owner had to leave town on some business and didn't want to leave his home unprotected, so he called our company and hired us to have someone here twenty-four-seven. Oh, and my name is August Day."

"August Day?" the cop asked, surprised.

"Yeah. August Day. My mother had a sense of humor, so when I was born, she named me August. She always told me she had a nice August Day every day."

The cop laughed. "Leave me your card so I know where to reach you if I have any more questions." Day pulled a business card from his pocket, wrote his cell phone number on it, and handed it to the detective. Day looked at the cop. "Look, could you arrange for one of your men to stay here until my relief arrives. He should be here any minute."

The detective turned to one of the policemen. "Artie."

"Yes, boss?"

"I want you to remain here until his relief gets here. Shouldn't be more than a few minutes. We don't want the house left unprotected. Understand?"

"Yep. Got it."

As the ambulance sped away with August Day aboard, Detective Yancy McGovern walked over to the detective who was busy examining the dead man.

"Did you find anything, Harry?"

"Yeah I did. His name is Joe Morte. *Morte?* That means 'death' in Italian. I guess this guy never figured on getting himself killed today, because I found his wallet on him with his ID and a wad of cash totaling—hold on while I count it. Let's see now. Yep, there's $2700 here."

"Bring the wallet over here. Let's have a look at what's in it. Maybe we'll get lucky and find out who sent him here. Driver's license and all the usual cards everyone carries. Wait a minute; here's something interesting." He held up a card and read it out loud. "Jean Lafitte Historical Society, Roger Claiborne President." McGovern rubbed his chin in deep thought. "What the hell is a card like this doing in this guy's wallet? I think we'll have to have a little talk with Mr. Roger Claiborne, President of the Jean Lafitte Historical Society."

Chapter 11

"Mr. Claiborne, there's a gentleman to see you."

"Does he have an appointment, Martha?"

"No, sir."

"Then arrange an appointment with him for tomorrow or the day after and tell him that I'm indisposed right now and can't see him."

"Sir . . . The man is a policeman from New York City and he flew all the way down here to see you."

Claiborne shifted in his seat uncomfortably. This couldn't be good news, he thought. "Oh. All right. Send him in."

Martha left the room and returned a few minutes later with Detective McGovern trailing behind her. Claiborne rose from his chair and greeted the detective.

"Good morning, Detective…"

"McGovern. Yancy McGovern. You are Roger Claiborne?"

"Yes, I am he. How can I be of assistance to you, Detective?"

"I won't waste your time. I'll be brief. Did you know a man by the name of Joseph Morte?"

"Joseph Morte, Morte." Claiborne snapped his fingers. "Yes, yes, now I remember. He was with a tour group that stopped here to visit the Jean Lafitte Blacksmith Shop. When they left, he stayed behind to ask me some questions."

McGovern's eyes widened. "Oh? He asked you some questions? About what, exactly?"

Meeting with this detective this morning wasn't part of Claiborne's plans and he had to think on his feet, which was always dangerous. He didn't want to dig himself a hole he couldn't get out of. Evasively, he continued with his explanation. "He wanted to know all about Jean Lafitte. I really don't have time to answer questions from every person who steps into Lafitte's old blacksmith shop."

"Blacksmith shop?"

Claiborne was treading on thin ice and he knew it; he had to get rid of this meddling detective before he said something he'd regret. "Yes. The Lafitte Blacksmith Shop is part of several tours, and the Jean Lafitte Historical Society makes a point of joining them at various times during the year. My grandfather and my father before me were presidents of the Jean Lafitte Historical Society and I have inherited that title from them. It goes back to our ancestor, who was Governor of Louisiana during the Lafitte era. It was on one of those tours that Mr. Morte asked about Lafitte."

The detective looked at his notes then jotted something down. "What exactly did he want to know about Lafitte?"

"He said he was doing research for a book and wanted to know about the Lafitte treasure."

"Treasure? I always thought that was a bunch of malarkey."

Claiborne smiled for the first time since the questioning began, but the smile vanished when the detective jotted something additional in his notepad. "No, the part about the treasure is true, but most of Lafitte's buried treasure has been found. I couldn't convince Mr. Morte that rumors of an undiscovered treasure were the figment of a romance writer's imagination. There is no treasure. That didn't discourage Morte, though. He asked if he could call me if he had any further questions, and I told him yes."

"Did you give him your card?"

"Why, yes. As a matter of fact, I did. May I ask why you are asking all these questions?"

Detective McGovern looked up from his notes and raised an eyebrow. "Mr. Morte was killed during a scuffle with a security guard after he broke into a home while the owner was away."

"Oh my goodness. I hope no one else was hurt."

"The guard was shot, but he'll recover. We searched Morte's body and found his wallet with your card in it and that's the reason for my visit."

"Oh, I see. It all makes sense now. As I just explained to you, Detective McGovern, I gave Mr. Morte my card and that is probably the card you're holding in your hand. But what was he doing breaking into a home?"

"That's just what I intend to find out, Mr. Claiborne. I may call you if I have any further questions."

"That's perfectly fine, Detective. Glad to be of service; call me anytime."

McGovern thanked Claiborne and left, but his sixth sense told him there was a lot more that Claiborne wasn't telling him.

As soon as McGovern left, Claiborne pulled out his throwaway cell phone and called a number. "Gerard, it's me, Roger. I must see you right away. I'll meet you at the cafe on the corner from my office in fifteen minutes. Is that enough time for you? Good. I'll see you in a few minutes, and then we'll talk."

McGovern had a feeling in his gut about Claiborne, so he walked to the corner, picked a spot where he had a clear view of Claiborne's office adjacent to the blacksmith shop and waited. His patience paid off as he watched Claiborne rush from the building and hurry down the street to the cafe on the corner, where he met another man. McGovern took out his iPhone and took a few pictures. They weren't very good because of the distance, but they managed to capture the essence of Claiborne and the man he met.

"Yes, that fool Morte got himself killed and now a New York City detective found my card and he came all the way down here to question me about it."

"Does he suspect anything?"

"No, I don't think so. I gave him a plausible explanation why the card was found on Morte's body."

"What did you tell him?"

"I said Morte told me he was doing research on Jean Lafitte's buried treasure and wanted information from me."

"Do you think he bought it?"

"What I think is that I whetted the cop's imagination when I brought up buried treasure. That should lead him back to Eddie Calto, and it's my guess he'll question Calto about Lafitte's buried treasure, and why a complete stranger was killed breaking into his house. The cop will want to know what Morte was looking for and why Calto left town so suddenly. I think Detective McGovern will have enough questions for Mr. Calto to keep him busy for a while. Take one of your men and fly up to New York. Do whatever you have to, but get the box from Calto. He has a girl with him now, and would you care to guess who her ancestor was?"

Gerard thought for a moment then tilted his head. "I have no idea. Why don't you tell me?"

"Pierre Lafitte, that's who. And my guess is the two of them know something, and they're pooling their information with the intention of splitting the treasure between them. That's what I think. And, Gerard?"

"Yes, boss."

"Calto is away and we don't know how long he'll be gone, so I suggest you wait four or five days before going to New York. Make sure you and the man with you leave your wallets and identification somewhere safe. If something were to happen to you, I don't want the police to identify you."

Chapter 12

u ms rmv!

"Are you going to try to remove the brick now?"

Eddie looked around without being obvious. "No . . . too many people are walking around here. We'll take a little stroll through the cemetery, but while we're walking let's keep our eyes on this tomb. When no one's near, we'll head back and I'll try to remove the brick. I'll have to stand on something, so if you spot anything I can use, let me know. Put your arm in mine and let's give the impression we're a young couple on our honeymoon."

Julianna liked that suggestion, so she eagerly put her arm through his. She even liked the thought being on their honeymoon. Looking at Eddie with a discerning eye, she liked what she saw. He was ruggedly handsome with a great profile. She wondered what his body was like, and squeezed his arm to get a sense of his musculature. It was firm and well-toned. She could just feel his masculinity radiating from him. How long had it been since she'd been with a man? Her mind wandered back to Jack, the young man she thought she was in love with. But the only thing he wanted from her was her virginity. And that was seven years ago. Seven years? My God, she thought. She looked up at Eddie and hoped he would make a pass at her, but she sensed he was too much of a gentleman for that.

She snuggled close and held onto his arm. They looked like lovers walking down the long corridor of tombs. At the end, they turned right and were about to venture up the next row when Eddie spotted a water faucet with a pail under it. To his delight, there was a trowel in it. Visitors used the pail and trowel to plant the flowers near a tomb and then water them. He picked up the pail and trowel and looked towards the tomb with the message on it.

"All clear. Let's head back and do this while no one's around." While they didn't run to the tomb, they did hurry. Eddie turned the pail over and, just as he was about to step on the pail holding the trowel, an elderly man and woman stepped from around the tomb, surprising Eddie. He did the first thing that came to mind. He grabbed Julianna and kissed her hard on her lips. To his surprise, she melted in his arms and returned his passionate kiss. This gave a whole new meaning to their search for Lafitte's treasure.

The elderly folks, seeing them embracing, realized they had interrupted two lovers. With knowing smiles they rushed away. But Eddie and Julianna's kisses lingered long after the elderly couple had left.

"Wow. I sure didn't mean for that to happen, but am I glad it did!" He looked at her. "I'm sorry, Julianna. I didn't know what else to do, so I did the first thing that came to mind. Am I forgiven?"

Julianna's face reddened, not knowing how to respond. She wanted to tell him how much she enjoyed the kiss, but didn't want to appear to be too easy. So instead, she gave him a big smile. "You're forgiven."

His smile lingered. "I wish I'd thought of that sooner and somewhere more private."

She laughed, blushing a deeper shade of red. "Your kiss surprised me, but I'm glad it happened."

It felt just like Eddie's birthday, and her kiss was the best present anyone in the world could have given him. He had kissed this girl and she liked it. This could be the beginning of a great romance.

He stepped on the pail and quickly inserted the trowel under the protruding brick. With a little prodding, it grated and then slipped from its nook. He stepped down from the pail and studied the brick, turning it over and over. He tried sprinkling water on it but, to his disappointment, there was nothing written on it. "Wait a minute." He stepped back on the pail, reaching into the empty slot. At first, he felt nothing. Then he pulled up the sleeve of his sweater and reached deeper into the opening. His heart beat a little faster as his fingers brushed against something. Reaching still further into the opening he caught something between his thumb and forefinger. He pulled from its two hundred-year-old hiding place a parchment wrapped in oilskin. "Julianna, hand me the brick." He slid the brick back in place so the tomb looked exactly as it did before. "Come on; let's get out of here. We found what we were looking for."

They took a cab back to the hotel and immediately went to Eddie's room. He washed his hands in the bathroom sink then went to the table where Julianna was waiting with the parchment. It was sealed with wax stamped with the familiar square and compass.

Eddie pointed to the bureau. "Julianna, get those two ashtrays and that bottle of wine and a glass." She wondered why he wanted a glass of wine now, but dutifully brought those items to the table. Eddie broke the seal on the parchment and—very slowly and carefully—unwrapped it. When it was unfurled, he placed the glass, the bottle and the two ashtrays on the corners. "Okay, let's see if we can interpret the code. Hand me that yellow pad."

1 luis, brgs u clsr. prd stl clsr- trd n mstr iln n rd ft. thr fnd krnkwa wmn sh ps t w. if nt t th sym pn fr th vl of ur o, tt of hvg ut t c a, ur t t o & br in th snd of th se at

lo wt mk whr th td ebs & fls twc i tw-f hrs

Julianna shook her head at the gibberish on the page. She couldn't make heads or tails of it. "What could this possibly mean?" She couldn't believe Eddie was actually smiling. "You know what this gibberish means, don't you?"

He nodded. "I can make out what some of it says, but the rest we'll have to take one step at a time. The first part is very confusing, but the second part is a simple Masonic code that refers to the third degree of Masonry, or the Master Mason's degree, so let's work on that part first."

if nt t th sym pn fr th vl of ur o, tt of hvg ut t c a, ur t t o & br in th snd of th se at lo wt mk whr th td ebs & fls twc i tw-f hrs

"I'm not sure about the first five words, but I'll have a go at the last part. Here goes:

For the violation of your oath, that of having your tongue cut out and you are taken to the ocean and buried in the sand of the sea at low water mark where the tide ebbs and flows twice in twenty-four hours.

"Let's see if I can get somewhere with the beginning of the code."

1 luis, brgs u clsr. prd stl clsr- trd n mstr iln. thr n rd ft fnd krnkwa wmn sh ps t w.

"'1 luis' must mean First St. Louis Cemetery. 'First St. Louis brings you closer.' That means we were successful in finding the first clue Lafitte hid behind the brick opening. 'Prd still closer?' What the hell does 'prd' represent? 'Tried in masters.' Masters what? And what does 'rd' mean? Road? Red? Ride? Julianna, I'm not getting anywhere with this. Please bring me my computer and let's do a Google search."

Eddie typed "Jean Lafitte" into Google and received 976,000 hits. He scanned through a number of pages until his eyes locked on 'pride.' The *Pride* was Lafitte's favorite ship; he even lived on it. Now the code was beginning to make sense. It said the *Pride* brought them still closer, so it could mean they might have to take a boat to find the next clue. "Trd in mstr iln thr n rd ft." He couldn't figure out what "trd" meant. But he figured the rest meant "in masters island near red fort."

"Julianna."

"Yes Eddie?"

"Where did Lafitte have his headquarters after the Battle of New Orleans?"

"It was either Barataria or Galveston. I'm not sure which."

After another quick Google search, he decided the code was pointing them to Barataria, because Galveston came a few years later.

thr fnd t krnkwa wmn sh ps t w

"There find the Karankawa woman. She points the way," he translated.

Julianna was confused. "Who is the Karankawa woman?"

"It's right here on Google. Here; read it for yourself."

After Lafitte's men kidnapped a Karankawa woman, warriors of her tribe attacked and killed five men of the colony. The corsairs aimed the artillery at the Karankawa, killing most of the men in the tribe.

Eddie looked at Julianna. "Lafitte included the last few

lines of the clue in the document to accomplish two things: 1. He wanted to confuse whoever found the parchment. 2. He wanted whoever discovered this clue to know that the clue had something to do with the sea.

"Now all we have to do is to find her grave and take it from there. There must be a statue or a memorial of some kind where Lafitte made sure she pointed to another clue, or even the treasure itself."

"Let's hope it's the latter she's pointing to. The treasure."

Chapter 13

Detective McGovern was taken upstairs to the captain's office by one of the firemen on duty. Captain Schieda offered the detective a seat, then he asked how he could be of assistance.

"I need some information concerning one of your firemen, Eddie Calto."

The captain raised his eyebrows a little upon hearing that. Captain Schieda was very protective of his men, especially Calto. "What do you want to know about him?"

"Has he gotten into any trouble while on the job? And, more specifically, has he made any enemies? Let me re-phrase that. Do you know of anyone who would want to hurt him?"

The captain became concerned. "Look, Detective, before I answer your questions, I want to know exactly what's going on here. Calto is, or I should say *was,* one of my best men . . . Dependable, reliable, honest, and one hell of a fireman. Did you know he was a hero while serving in the army in Iraq?"

The detective shook his head. "I didn't know that. He sounds like quite a guy."

"He is. Now why don't you level with me, Detective, and tell me what's going on with Eddie."

"Someone was killed while trying to break into his home. The intruder expected the house to be empty. But he was surprised to find a security guard that Calto had hired."

"What was the name of the man who was killed?"

"Joseph Morte."

The captain shook his head. "Never heard of him. Please continue."

"Well, there's not much more to tell. The guard was shot, but the intruder was killed during the struggle. He was dead when we arrived at the scene. We found identification in his wallet."

"Was there any clue as to who hired him?"

The detective shook his head. "Not really. There was a business card in the wallet, and I just got back from a wild goose chase in New Orleans. It was the only lead I had."

Captain Schieda shifted in his chair. "New Orleans, you say?"

Now it was the detective's turn to shift in his seat. "Yeah. Why?"

"One of my men, Frank Scaffo, returned a medal to Eddie that he'd forgotten in his locker. While he was in Eddie's home, Eddie introduced him to a young lady. Frank said she was a direct descendant of Pierre Lafitte. If I remember my history, the Lafittes had their base of operation in New Orleans."

Detective McGovern pulled Claiborne's card from his pocket and handed it to Captain Schieda. "This is the card I found in the dead man's wallet. It appears that our Mr. Claiborne may not be the upstanding citizen he pretends to be." McGovern stood. "You've been a great help, Captain. When I came in here, I was grasping at straws, hoping you might be able to help me. Well, you've connected some of the dots for me and that sheds a whole new light on this case." The two men shook hands and McGovern left to do some additional research on Jean Lafitte, his brothers, and his treasure. Captain Schieda watched from his second-story window as Detective McGovern drove away. Then he picked up the phone and telephoned Calto on his cell phone.

Chapter 14

"Well, Julianna, that's enough work for one night." Eddie smiled, put his hands on her shoulders, and motioned toward the door. "Come on; let's get dressed and go to dinner, and afterwards we'll find a nice club where we'll enjoy a drink, maybe share a dance or two, and just relax. God knows, we deserve it."

Julianna slipped into a beautiful, low-cut lavender dress that showed a lot of cleavage. She'd brought it with her from St. Louis hoping she'd have a chance to wear it. She got her wish and wanted to feel sexy tonight.

Eddie wore a pair of black Italian slacks, a white silk shirt, and a grey suede sports jacket. He felt good tonight. He was going to dinner with a beautiful woman and he was looking forward to sitting at a secluded table in a nice little club, enjoying a drink and sharing a dance or two with Julianna. He needed to relax and this lady was allowing him to do just that . . . relax.

Julianna came from her room and looked just beautiful. Eddie took her by the arm and walked her to the elevator. In the lobby, Eddie asked the concierge where the dining room was. As the couple walked past the fine shops that lined the walkway leading to the dining room, Eddie noticed a jewelry store and whispered to Julianna, "Come in here with me for a moment."

Julianna was surprised. "Why are we stopping in here?"

"Because, although you look enchanting in that sexy dress you're wearing, there's something missing."

She looked down at her dress. "Something is missing?"

"Yes, now come over to this counter. I've spotted what's missing." He called the clerk over and pointed to a necklace. "Let me see that necklace." The clerk reached. "No not that one. The one next to it."

Julianna gasped. It was a magnificent diamond necklace.

"Let's see how it looks on you."

Julianna looked in the mirror and started to cry.

"Hey! What are you crying about?"

"It's just that I never had anything so beautiful to wear around my neck."

Eddie looked at the clerk. "We'll take it. Put the necklace on, and lay the box in your purse. Then let's go to dinner. I'm starved."

"But . . . don't you want to know the price?"

"Nope." Eddie paid the bill with his credit card, and then the couple headed towards the restaurant.

"Eddie, you didn't have to do this. I mean, it's so expensive."

"Yeah, I know, and you know what?"

"No. What?"

"A couple of months ago I couldn't have afforded the hotel bill, but now that I can have anything I want, why not spend the money on someone I like?"

She stopped walking and looked at him, her moist eyes glistening with tears. "You like me?"

He smiled. "Yes. I do like you."

"You like me a lot?"

"Yes a lot."

Julianna threw her arms around him and kissed him hard on the lips. "I like you a lot too. Now look what I did. I ruined my lipstick."

Eddie pointed to the ladies' room. "Go on and fix your face. I'll wait here."

Five minutes later, Julianna returned and held him by the

arm. "Come on; let's get dinner and enjoy our night together."

Eddie liked the sound of that. It promised to be an interesting and exciting night. Dinner was delectable.

"Are you ready for the nightclub and a few drinks?" Eddie asked, after paying the bill.

She looked at him with misty eyes. "Why don't we have our drinks in our room? I think I'd like that better. Don't you agree?"

They stepped from the elevator and walked back to their suite hand in hand like two lovers. At the door, Eddie surprised her by picking her up and carrying her over the threshold. She giggled contentedly and nestled her head in his shoulder. He walked through to the bedroom and placed her gently on his bed. "No," she said. "Not yet. Mix us a drink first while I change."

"What drink do you prefer?"

"I don't care. A gin and tonic or a rum and Coke; either is good." She finally settled for a gin and tonic.

"Good. I'll make one for each of us."

Ten minutes later, the door to Julianna's room opened and she walked out, wearing a very sexy Victoria's Secret negligée and a sheer silk robe that left very little to the imagination. She didn't say anything as she approached him; she just took her drink, tilted it in his direction, and tapped his glass lightly. "Here's to us, and our quest for the treasure."

Eddie raised his drink. "Here, here."

They each took a sip, then Eddie put his drink on the bureau. She let him take her drink and place it beside his. He took her in his arms and kissed her tenderly, and she responded by pressing herself against him tightly. His hardness pressing against her aroused her passion and she couldn't wait to feel him inside her. He pushed her gently away and he took off his shirt. She gasped at the magnificence of his body. She hadn't expected him to be in such good shape. He in turn marveled at the perfect curves of her body. He slid off her robe and let it fall to the ground; then he did the same with her negligée. It was now his turn to gasp at the perfect curves of her full body. Her breasts were perfectly full and round and her nipples were erect in expectation of desires yet to be fulfilled. They slid under the covers and pulled close to one another. He explored her body with his hands, and when he reached down and traced his fingers along her thigh she shuddered and responded by reaching for his manhood. She started stroking him. It had been a long, long time for Julianna and she was savoring this moment as she guided him into her. She loved being with Eddie. It was as if she had waited her whole life for this man. She had only known him a few days and, for the first time in her life, she was hopelessly in love. Eddie was everything she had ever wanted or dreamed about in a man.

Chapter 15

Unbeknownst to Roger Claiborne, Eddie Calto and Julianna Montaigne were in New Orleans and just leaving their hotel about one thousand feet from his office.

"Where are we going?" Julianna asked Eddie.

"I checked with the hotel concierge and there's a helicopter charter service located at the Louie Armstrong New Orleans International Airport. I want to take a cab to the airport and charter a chopper to take us to Barataria. Are you up for this?"

"Try and keep me away," she replied with a good-natured smile on her beautiful face.

As he waved for a cab, he looked over at her. "Have I told you lately that you're beautiful?"

"No," she said still smiling.

"Well, I'll say it now. You are one beautiful woman. By the way, how was last night for you?"

She shrugged her shoulders. "Oh, it was passable, but only just so."

He joined in her laughter. "Oh is that so? Well, tonight, I'll just have to try harder."

Julianna became serious for a moment. "Eddie."

"Yeah," he said while still trying to hail a cab.

"Last night was the most wonderful night of my life. I have never enjoyed myself as much as I did last night with you. From the wonderful meal in the hotel to the dessert in your bed. It was wonderful."

Eddie was touched. He was about to say something when a cab pulled up and the driver reached over and opened the

back door. "Where to?"

"Louie Armstrong New Orleans International Airport. Do you know where the helicopter charter service is located?"

"Sure, no problem. I'll drop you off in front of the place."

"Good, then let's get the show on the road."

A little while later the cab stopped in front of Kenner Helicopter Charters.

Eddie chartered a helicopter for the day. The going rate per hour was $1348, but Eddie offered the pilot $8500 to hire him for the day. The pilot checked his schedule and had no other clients, so he accepted Eddie's offer. He'd remain with his two fares for the day. The pilot gave the couple a set of head phones each, explaining they could communicate better over the noise of the engine. The pilot sounded like Chubby while he was giving the First St. Louis Cemetery tour spiel. Mark, the pilot, pointed out various landmarks along the way. He explained that Barataria was fifteen miles long and about twelve miles wide and was situated in southeastern Louisiana. "You know," he said with pride as they began their descent, "Barataria Island was once the home base of Jean Lafitte, the notorious pirate; he made it his base after the War of 1812. Now, where do you want me to drop you off?"

"Do you happen to know where Lafitte's two-story red house was located?"

"Yeah, but it's no longer there."

"Drop us as close as possible to where the house was located. This young lady is related to Pierre Lafitte and she wants to familiarize herself with her ancestors' hangouts and properties for a book she's writing."

"Oh, okay. I'll drop you off close to where the house was located and you can take your time and look around. I'm yours for the day, so I won't be going anywhere. While you're gone I'll sit and read my book."

"Thanks, we appreciate it."

Once they had landed, Eddie became confused by the terrain. "Say, where would we find the remains of Lafitte's old headquarters?"

Mark pointed toward a hill. Lafitte's house had been on the highest point of the island. "From what little I've heard from the tour guides, Lafitte wanted to make sure he could see a ship entering his waters before it got too close. You'll find a marker up there where his house used to be."

Eddie reached for a satchel under the seat and he and Julianna trudged up the hill in the direction Mark had pointed. When they reached the highest point, which wasn't very high considering the flatness of the island, they came upon a marker that read, "Jean Lafitte, the famous pirate's house was located on this spot." Eddie scratched his head. "Now all we have to do is find the Karankawa woman's statue. The problem is, I don't know where to look."

Julianna thought a moment then said, "If Lafitte expected someone to find the Karankawa woman with the clues he left behind, he wouldn't have made it that difficult. What he would have made difficult is the clue she carried and not her statue, so she has to be somewhere close. Come on; let's take a walk around the area and see what we can find."

Eddie nodded his agreement. "Let's see now. If the front of his house was facing the sea, it stands to reason that's where he would have placed the Karankawa woman."

They walked twenty paces down toward the furrowed and marshy water that overlooked the bay. From that vantage point, Eddie scanned the horizon to see the many small islands in the surrounding low-lying Barataria Country, just a short distance south of New Orleans ... and that was when they saw her. She was approximately six feet tall and had aged remarkably well. The marble block she was carved from was still in very good condition. Her right arm was outstretched, pointing in the direction of the sea—as if she were pointing to her kidnappers. Her face, while beautiful, wore a stern, accusing gaze of contempt. Her left arm extended at an angle by her side, away from her body.

"Look!" Julianna said. "She's pointing toward the distance, and it seems to me she's pointing to nothing in particular, just the water. I don't understand what she could be pointing at."

Eddie was unsure. "Let's take a look around the area. Maybe a storm or possibly a curator unwittingly moved the statue, or turned it so it's facing the wrong way. Let's see the other potential spots she might have been pointing to."

They searched for a clue, but after half an hour walking in circles, Julianna expressed what they were both feeling. "It's hopeless. There's nothing here that she could be pointing to."

Eddie agreed. "Come on; let's go back to her and see if there are other secrets she may be hiding. Maybe the clue is inside the statue?" Then he thought better of it. "No, that would be impossible. She's carved from a solid block of marble. Well . . . let's go back and take another look anyway. Who knows? Maybe we'll see something we missed the first time." They walked back to the statue and followed her arm with their eyes as she pointed away from land to nowhere in particular. "This doesn't make any sense," Eddie mused. "Hey wait a minute," Eddie said gleefully. "We've been looking at this all wrong."

Julianna perked up. "What do you mean?"?

He laughed out loud. "Because we're looking at the wrong arm. Her left arm is pointing to the clue!" The Karankawa woman's left arm was hanging away from her body at a sixty-five-degree angle, pointing to a spot about fifteen feet from where she stood. Eddie pulled a laser pointer from his bag and sighted it along the angle of her arm. The red dot pointed to a spot near a copse of trees. Eddie glanced around to make sure no one was near. From the satchel he took a small military-type shovel, the kind that folds, making it easier to carry. He dug down about three feet. It was hard going, and he found nothing. He was beginning to think he may have misread the message, but he continued digging another foot. Still nothing. It was tiring work. He thought about trying another spot, but figured since he had dug this far down, he may as well dig another foot before giving up. So he plunged the shovel hard into the ground and, to his surprise and delight, he hit something metallic. He dug around the object: an oblong box. He pulled it free and yanked it to the grassy surface. Then, he replaced the dirt, patting it down to make it hard for anyone to know a hole had been dug there.

Meanwhile Julianna, making sure no one was watching, placed the metal box and the shovel in the satchel. After the hole was covered, Eddie brushed himself off, walked up to the Karankawa woman and kissed her on the cheek. "Thanks, old girl; you did your job well." Then, he and Julianna made their way back down the hill, where they found Mark sitting on a fold up chair, reading a book near his helicopter.

Chapter 16

McGovern stopped by a cubicle in the 6th precinct in Queens. "Helen, did you get me the information on Claiborne I asked for?"

"Yeah, I placed it on your desk."

"Anything interesting I should know about?"

"Well, it's kinda strange. It appears that during Lafitte's time, the governor of Louisiana was William C. C. Claiborne. And after the battle of New Orleans, the Lafitte brothers were national heroes, especially in New Orleans. When the Jean Lafitte Historical Society was initially formed, every generation of Claiborne's ancestors became the chairman of that society. What struck me as very odd was that Governor Claiborne hated Lafitte and, if he hated him, why would he want his ancestors to be associated with him, and especially become President of Lafitte's historical society? It makes you wonder, doesn't it?"

McGovern rubbed his chin. "Yeah, it sure does. It makes you wonder what their motives were. It almost looks as if they were waiting for something to happen. It looks as though something did. I don't know exactly what, but I think that Calto and Claiborne are both in it up to their ears. I can't figure out what set this whole thing off."

Helen's eyes narrowed. "Set what off, Yancy?"

"Well, for one thing, Calto has come into a large inheritance. Oh, that's all legal like. I checked it out. His great-great-grandfather left the inheritance for him. But as soon as he gets it, it seems people are trying to kill him. Take that guy, Joe Morte, who broke into Calto's. Then I find Claiborne's card in the dead guy's wallet. The treasure Lafitte hid just before the Battle of New Orleans was purported to be enormous.

"I think Claiborne set this whole charade up back in the early 1800s, figuring that sooner or later, Lafitte's heirs would look for his treasure. And Claiborne hated Lafitte so much that he figured, why should Lafitte's heirs get the treasure? If his heirs were diligent, they could be there to take it and keep it for themselves. That's my theory and that's what I'm basing my investigation on. I'm worried about that Calto kid though. He seems like a good guy. His captain told me he's a decorated army veteran, an FDNY medal winner, and he's patriotic. But I think he's gonna get hurt unless I can figure out a way to prevent it. Well, maybe the answer is in the report you left on my desk."

"Could be, Yancy. There's a lot of material there." Helen turned back to her computer and quickly became lost in her thoughts as she typed away on her keyboard.

* * *

Eddie laid the metal box in the bathtub and washed it with a damp rag. Dirt and sediment had accumulated all over it while it lay buried these past two centuries. When the box was as clean as he could get it, he turned it over and checked the seam on the cover. It was sealed with wax, probably to keep the moisture out. Pretty smart of Lafitte, he thought. He pulled his Randall 15 Airman's knife from the leather scabbard on his belt and began carefully to chip away the wax that sealed and protected the box. He had always carried this knife with him in the army, and then in the FDNY. He had wrapped it in a T-shirt, placed it in his luggage, and checked it aboard the plane when he flew down to New Orleans.

When all the wax was removed, he tried opening the box,

but it stubbornly resisted all his efforts. He took the knife and placed the edge of the strong blade under the cover, and gently teasing it upwards until, with a resisting groan, it squeaked open. Inside, they discovered a single page of loosely rolled parchment. The page was sealed with what appeared to be the same wax used to seal the metal cover, except this seal had an imprint of the now very familiar Masonic square and compass stamped onto it. Eddie removed the parchment reverently and carried it to the table, being very careful how he handled it. After all the years underground, he was afraid the paper would disintegrate when he opened it. But he needn't have worried; the paper was remarkably well preserved, considering the dampness and rain that soaked into the ground around the little box. It had somehow managed to survive in excellent condition.

"Let's do this right," Eddie told Julianna. "There are plastic gloves in my bag. Would you please take out two pairs. Let's put them on before handling this delicate paper. I should have put them on before handling the parchment, but it's too late to worry about that now."

Julianna gave Eddie one pair, and put one on herself. Then Eddie reached for his trusty Randall and gently cut through the seal, freeing the parchment. He carefully opened the letter, spread it out on the table, and secured it with two glasses and a book. While the parchment was a full page, the writing on it was minimal. "Another riddle. Man . . . I hope that this is the last one."

Julianna was excited. "What does it say, Eddie?"

"Well for one thing, it's written in the same Masonic code the others were written in, only this one is a little more complicated. Get that pad over on the credenza and write down what I tell you."

She retrieved the pad and took out her pen. "I'm ready whenever you are."

"Write down these letters in the sequence I give them to you."

on d o mo oly wn t rb s fl wl gd svnt c u sw lt f rls nd ll w b urs.

Julianna read it and shook her head. "I have no idea what that means. I hope you have better luck figuring it out than I do."

"Let's see. Okay, write what I tell you. I may have to change a word or two after I finish, but we have to start somewhere. Wait, don't write yet. 'On.' I think that means 'one.' The next word together with the first word could mean 'on date' or 'on day'—no, I think it means 'One day.' Okay, write down 'one day.' Now the 'o' and 'mo.' 'O' must mean 'of.' Write down 'of month' next to 'one day.' We have 'one day of month' so far. 'Oly wn t rb s fl,' I believe, is 'only when the orb is full.'"

"What the heck does that mean? When the orb is full?" Julianna sighed.

Eddie laughed. "Don't you see? The orb is the moon and Lafitte is telling us that we only have one day of the month to do whatever it is that we have to do. We can only do it when the moon is full. Let's see what else he's telling us. I think I have it. 'Will God's servant see you.' God's servant must mean a priest. The following words are a little more difficult to interpret. Let's seeeee. Write down 'Show letter' . . . Now what does the 'f' mean. Of? For? I think it means 'of.' I don't know what 'rls' means, but the rest says, 'All will be yours.' 'Rls' has to mean 'release.' Now read it back."

"'One day of the month only when the orb is full will God's servant see you. Show letter of release and all will be yours.' But what or where is the letter of release?"

Eddie took the paper and put it to the light to see if there were any words hidden in the parchment. Nothing! He lit a match to see if the heat would reveal anything written in invisible ink, but there was nothing. "This is gonna drive me crazy. Where the hell would Lafitte have hidden the letter of release? Let's start from the beginning with what we have. All the codes we found have led us to this box and this parchment. This is all we have, so it stands to reason that if the letter of release is not written on the parchment, it's either written on the box somewhere or it's hidden in the box." He turned the box over and examined every bit of the metal bottom, but there was nothing written on it. He re-opened the box and examined it carefully. He reached down, pulled out his knife, and ran the tip of it around the edge of the bottom of the box. "There may be a false bottom; at least I hope there is," he said without much conviction. "This box has been under the ground for so long that if there's a false bottom, it's rusted solid."

Eddie figured that the outside of the box would be much more difficult to work loose than the inside, so he decided to work from within the box. He took his knife and pressed it into the bottom seam. He felt a little give, so he moved the knife a little further down the seam, wiggled it in, and pried the bottom a little more. He was rewarded with a little more give. "I think there is a false bottom to this box, Julianna. It's beginning to give a little." He did the same thing to the other end. The bottom of the box began to peel upwards about an inch. A little more, and he would be able to get his fingers under the metal and lift it free. He kept working the blade, loosening the false bottom, until it finally broke free. He discovered why it was so difficult to open. It was sealed with wax, giving the impression that it was one solid metal bottom. Very clever, Eddie thought. He had a lot more respect for Lafitte now. Beneath the false bottom was a packet with the square and compass pressed into the wax seal. He carefully broke the seal, opened the packet and pulled out the contents. There were three sheets of parchment in the package. The top sheet contained instructions.

To have gotten this far, you must have found and deciphered all the codes I left. Now you must follow the instructions and take the enclosed letter to the prior and not to any priests; only the prior of the First St. Louis Cathedral, and only on the day stated in the coded instructions. The pastor will ask three questions and you must answer them correctly. The first question he will ask is: Where you are coming from? You will answer: From the west, traveling to the east. The second question he will ask is: Why are you traveling to the east? Your answer will be: In order to gain more knowledge and enlightenment. The third and final question he will ask is: Are you worthy of this great honor that you are about to receive? Your answer will be: I am. I have taken a sacred vow never to abuse this great honor under the penalty of death. Remember, if you go to the pastor on any day but when the orb is full, his door will be closed to you.

With those three questions answered correctly, you will be taken to a repository where the treasure waits for the widow's son.

Eddie wiped his brow with his sleeve. "Wow, this guy was something else. What the hell could he have hidden to make him go to this much trouble?"

"I don't know, but maybe the letter of release will shed some light."

Eddie picked up the letter and read it out loud.

August 29, 1814

To the pastor of the First St. Louis Cathedral:

The bearer of this letter comes to you as a friend, but your duty is to determine if this person is qualified to be given the items you have kept safe in the repository of your church in a location of your choosing and known only to you. To claim the prize, he must prove worthy and well qualified by correctly answering three questions, which only you, the current prior of this church will know. If he answers the questions correctly, you will then assist him in retrieving that which was given to you for safekeeping. Then you will do all in your power to see that he is taken safely to a place of his choosing and protected from thieves and ruffians who may seek to take what he has rightly earned. When your task is completed, the vigilance you and your brother priors have maintained through the years will have come to an end.

Jean Lafitte.

Chapter 17

That night, Eddie had an uneasy feeling he was being followed. He feared his enemies had come to New York to find him and, when they discovered he wasn't there, he surmised they might have rushed back to New Orleans, because this is where the treasure was hidden. He hoped he was wrong, but he usually trusted his instincts. They had never proved wrong before.

Though it was still dark, he went into the kitchen and put on a pot of coffee. He poured himself a cup, and walked past Julianna as she lay on the bed fast asleep. He went quietly out onto the balcony where he could think clearly. The room was at the very top of the building, so he knew he'd be safe from anyone observing him. He leaned back in his chair and rested his feet on the outside railing, sipping his coffee and trying to make sense of all that Julianna and he had been through. One thing became clear to him. They had been here too long. It was time to leave.

He was preparing to get up from the comfortable lounge chair and turned to put his coffee cup on the table beside him. Just as he placed the cup on the table, it shattered. Eddie's old army instincts kicked in and he ducked as another shot whizzed by him, shattering the glass door leading into the bedroom, awakening Julianna. Eddie ran into the room and dived onto the bed on top of Julianna, pulling her with him as he rolled off the other side of the bed and onto the floor.

"They're probably using a rifle with an infrared scope," he whispered. "If we stay here it'll give them time to sight in on us. Our best chance of surviving is to make a run for the living room away from the windows."

They reached over and grabbed their clothes from the chair beside the bureau behind which they were hiding. On Eddie's signal, they dashed across the room to the safety of the living room as shots were fired harmlessly behind them.

Julianna was frightened and she pulled Eddie close and held him tightly. "Who exactly is 'they'?"

Eddie replayed in his mind the call he had received from Captain Schieda, telling him about McGovern's visit to the firehouse and Claiborne's card, and the conversation they had concerning McGovern's trip to New Orleans. So Eddie put two and two together and concluded there must be a connection between the card and the gunshots, which meant that Claiborne was somehow involved.

"If I had to take a guess, I'd say it was Claiborne or one of his men. Come on; let's get dressed and get out of here while we still can."

They dressed quickly. Eddie held Julianna and looked directly into her eyes. "There's nothing here that we can't replace, so just leave everything. Understand?" Julianna nodded. "Good. I'll just take the MacBook Pro and Lafitte's letters. Now come on; let's get out of here before we have visitors." They raced to the elevator and took it to the second floor.

"This is not the lobby. Why are we getting off here?"

"There may be bad guys waiting for us by the elevator in the lobby. It's safer if we walk down the exit stairs and have a look around before we step out onto the main floor."

They walked quickly down the stairs. Eddie motioned for her to stay there while he opened the door a crack to see if it was safe to leave. "Okay; it looks clear. We'll head out the rear exit and take a cab to the church." Eddie stopped in his tracks.

"What's wrong?"

"Damn. I forgot. We can't go to the church now."

"Why not?"

"It's not a full moon. The pastor would never give us anything if we approached him on the wrong day. We'll have to hide out somewhere for the next few days."

Julianna was becoming nervous. "Where can we hide? If whoever shot at us found us here, they'll find us no matter where we go."

"Maybe, maybe not. We'll just have to be smart and think things out. I'll rent us a car and find us a safe place to hide out for a few days."

They left the hotel through the service entrance and ran to the cab stop, located just a few doors from the rear exit. "Take us to the airport."

The driver turned on the meter and sped away.

"Why are we going to the airport?"

Eddie whispered so the cabbie couldn't hear what he was saying. "If the bad guys have connections in the cab companies, they'll know we were taken to the airport, and maybe they'll get the idea that we were taking a flight back to New York. Meanwhile, we'll find a small hotel on the outskirts of New Orleans and stay there for a few days."

"Do you think we'll be safe there, Eddie?"

"I really don't know. I think so, but we can't dwell on what might or might not happen. We can't leave until we locate the treasure that's so valuable people are willing to kill to get it. I know it's difficult, but let's try to relax and just look forward to finding the treasure. Look how far we've come. We've solved all the clues, and now all we have to do is wait until the moon is full and go talk to the pastor. So just hang in there a little while longer. Then we'll go to Europe and we'll tour all the great cities. It'll be fun; you wait and see."

"Oh, Eddie. I hope we live long enough to enjoy it."

"We will. You have my promise on that."

She turned to him and smiled. "That's what I love about you, Eddie. You are the eternal optimist."

"Here we are, folks. Which terminal are you looking for?"

"Take us to the Delta terminal, please." Eddie paid the man and left him a generous tip, then he and Julianna stepped into the terminal and looked for the car rental agencies. At the Avis counter, he asked the young lady if she had a high-end car available.

"We have a BMW 750 available."

Without asking the price, Eddie said, "We'll take it." Rather than hand her a credit card, he paid in cash. But the woman asked for his credit card anyway to keep the number on file. He hoped Claiborne wasn't technically savvy enough to trace credit card purchases. The woman gave him instructions on where to find the car, and he smiled. "We're on our honeymoon," he told her, "and we'd prefer not to stay in one of those fancy hotels in town. Would you happen to know of a small, romantic motel where we can spend a few days alone without being disturbed?"

The young lady smiled. "I know just the place. It's about fifteen miles out of town. It's very private and many newlyweds go there."

"It sounds perfect."

She handed Eddie a map and circled the hotel's location. Eddie slipped her a twenty-dollar tip and winked at her. "Thanks. You alone could be responsible for making our stay in New Orleans memorable." The girl blushed, wishing it were she that was going with him to that motel.

Chapter 18

"What do you mean you missed them, Cleon? If you had killed them, I could have gone up to their room and just taken what I'm looking for. I know they found something, but I have no idea what it is or where they went."

Cleon, in an attempt to rise in his boss's estimation, clamored, "I checked with the cab companies and spread some money around and I got lucky. I had to shell out some bucks, but it was worth it because one cabbie told me he took a man and a woman to the airport and dropped them off at the Delta terminal."

"You fool," Claiborne bellowed. "I hope you didn't scare them off and force them to leave town. If they left town, it will make it that much more difficult to get what I want from them, especially if the police get involved. Come on; let's go."

"Where are we going, boss?"

"To the airport. I want to check all the flight manifests from New Orleans to New York. They didn't leave on a Delta flight, that's for sure," said Claiborne.

At the airport they checked with all the airlines, but they had left on none of them.

Claiborne sat down and reflected. "You know, I think they tried to make it look like they left and they're still in New Orleans. Hmm . . . but where would they go? Where would they feel safest staying here? And the big question is . . . If they found the treasure, why didn't they leave New Orleans? Why are they still hanging around here?"

Cleon rubbed his chin. "Maybe the treasure is too big to take with them."

"No, Cleon. My ancestor left his future heirs a trust, and in it he said he had word that Lafitte left clues to the treasure. Maybe they haven't found it yet. That must be it. Maybe we've overestimated them. Come on. You and the boys are going to start checking all the hotels and motels in and around New Orleans."

* * *

Julianna and Eddie decided to take one room to make it appear that they were newlyweds. "This motel is perfect. It's fifteen miles out of town and I think that's far enough out that Claiborne won't be able to find us. But we can't take anything for granted; we can't let our guard down."

Julianna yawned and stretched her arms. "What are we supposed to do now? We still have three days before the full moon."

Eddie wore the shadow of a smile as he put his arms around her. He whispered in her ear, "I know exactly how we can pass the time without becoming bored."

She laughed and whispered back, "Without knowing exactly what you have in mind, I know I'm going to love it."

They made love passionately, trying desperately to release the tension in their bodies after having been stalked and chased around New Orleans by faceless men who wanted to steal their secret, even if it meant killing them for it.

"Eddie let's do something. I'm getting hungry. Let's go out to dinner and, maybe afterward, we could take in a movie."

"Sounds good."

They asked the desk clerk what restaurant he recommended, and where the movie theatre was. He recommended a small Cajun roadhouse about half a mile down the road.

The dinner was surprisingly good and, while the two lovers enjoyed their meal, they noticed that the people in the place looked as though they came right out of *Duck Dynasty*. There were a lot of rough-looking characters.

"Come on; let's get out of here."

They paid their bill and stepped out into the dark night. Julianna looked at her watch.

"We still have another hour to kill before the movie starts. Let's go across the street and have a drink while we wait."

"That sounds like a good idea. I could use a drink." They entered the bar, which was nothing more than a roadhouse-type bar. All eyes were on the pretty lady with the well-built dude. They took a table in the corner away from the throng and waited for the waitress.

"What'll y'all have?"

"Gin and tonic," said Julianna.

"I'll have a rum and Coke," Eddie added. The drinks came and they conversed amiably, discussing what they would do after they found the treasure, when a large man approached their table.

"They're playing our song, darlin'. I'd like to have this dance with you."

Julianna shook her head and pasted a smile on her face. "Thank you, but no. I'm in the middle of a conversation with my husband and it wouldn't be fair to him if I danced with you."

The large man grinned, showing a few missing teeth in his ugly face. "You must have misunderstood me. I didn't ask you to dance. I'm telling you that you are going to dance with me."

His friends were all leering at him with shit-eating grins on their faces. "Go on, Edgar. Make her dance with you."

Eddie looked up at the man. "Look, friend. We don't want any trouble with you. We're sitting here, minding our own business, enjoying a drink before we go to the movies."

Julianna grew nervous. She watched Eddie's face, but he didn't seem the least bit nervous, even with this brute standing so close to them.

Eddie's combat training came into play. He realized he was within this guy's punching range and knew he had to put some distance between them before the guy sucker punched him. But he couldn't do it sitting down. "Excuse me, honey, I have to stand for a minute."

The big guy turned to his friends and pointed at Eddie. "He's gotta stand for a minute. That's because he probably pissed in his pants." His friends thought this was hysterical. They were laughing so hard they were holding their sides. Eddie stood and turned his back to Edgar as if he were about to walk away but, instead, he turned so quickly that even Julianna was stunned by his move. Eddie turned and, with all his force, punched Edgar in the solar plexus, knocking the wind out of him. Then, with his left hand, he lifted Edgar's head by the hair and, with his right hand, hit him right on the sweet spot of his chin, knocking him clear across the room, where he fell over a table, causing the two men drinking there to scurry out of the way. Edgar got up wearily and shook his head in an attempt to clear it. He realized he had just been made a fool of. He bellowed in rage and ran towards Eddie, who was just about to leave the place with Julianna in hand. But, seeing that this wasn't going away, he told Julianna to wait outside.

Edgar was in a blind fury and charged recklessly at Eddie with his ham like fists closed, ready to pound Eddie into chopped meat. Just as he was about to slam him, Eddie stepped aside and grabbed his hand, as he was taught to do by both his hand-to-hand combat instructor in the service, and his sensei at his dojo. He spun Edgar around so that he made a somersault in the air and landed hard, flat on his back. Eddie jumped on Edgar and was about to crush his larynx, but Julianna, who had been watching, horrified, screamed out, "No, Eddie don't do it! Don't do it!"

Eddie caught himself and was about to get up when a chair crashed down on his back. He rolled over and sprang to his feet, wary of who hit had him. Two of Edgar's friends were glaring at him. "Look, guys, you don't have to do this. He started it, and all we want to do is leave this place. We don't want any more trouble."

One of the men snarled, "You just busted the hornet's nest, and now you're gonna git stung. Come on, Clem; he can't take on both of us." The men rushed Eddie, who tried to dodge out of the way; but with two men coming at him, he had nowhere to go. Instead, he remembered the words of Bruce Lee. "Use your foot because that puts the most distance between you and your attacker." That was just what Eddie did. He waited for the men to rush him and, in that moment, he spin-kicked and hit one of the men on the chin, knocking him to the floor, unconscious for the moment. Now it was just him and Clem.

"You don't have to do this. There's been enough trouble, Clem, I don't want to hurt you."

There was doubt on Clem's face. He looked at Edgar, who was lying unconscious on the ground, and then he looked over at Harvey, who was wobbling as he attempted to get to his feet. He put his fists down and backed away. "Go on," Clem warned. "You better get out of here while you still can. The sheriff is Edgar's brother and Doris, your waitress, called him when the fight broke out, so you better be goin' now if you don't want to wind up in jail, 'cause he'll be here any minute. You hear!"

"Thanks for letting me know."

Clem smiled. "It's nothin'. But you better be goin' now, hear. You don't want the sheriff to get his hands on you, 'cause he's not a very gentle man, you hear?"

"I hear and thanks." Eddie grabbed Julianna's hand and they raced to their car and sped off to their motel. "Grab your stuff. We're getting out of here. I have a feeling the sheriff will be here any moment." Both Julianna and Eddie put their things hurriedly in their bags and rushed to their car and, in another minute, they were on their way out of town.

Eddie maintained the speed limit as he drove down the dark, lonely road that headed back to New Orleans. Then, suddenly, the night lit up behind them as the flashing lights of the sheriff's car illuminated the inside of their car, and a voice over the loudspeaker commanded them to pull over.

Chapter 19

The sheriff arrested Eddie and charged him with starting a brawl in a local tavern. Julianna wasn't charged with any crime, because she wasn't involved in the fracas, so she was released. The following morning, she went to the jail to visit Eddie and was shocked by his condition. He had been brutally beaten. Julianna turned to the sheriff. "Who did this to him?"

The sheriff smiled venomously at her. "I did. He resisted arrest, so he had to be restrained."

Before Julianna could say anything, a deputy came and whispered something to the sheriff, who nodded. The two officers left the room. Eddie was lying pathetically on the cot and not moving. He was unconscious but breathing steadily. She left the cell area and walked into the waiting room. She had a mind to have words with the sheriff before leaving, post bail for Eddie and get him out of there as quickly as possible. Then she would get him to a hospital for x-rays and proper treatment. He could have broken ribs, a concussion, and God knows what else internally wrong with him after the sheriff's beating. While she waited, a deputy walked out of the sheriff's office and, through the open door, she saw a well-dressed man talking to the sheriff. But what shocked her was the name on the door. *Horace B. Claiborne, Sheriff.* The man in the suit could be Claiborne himself! She rose quickly and walked quietly out of the building. She got in the rental car and drove around the block, parking up the street where she had a good view of the jail. She waited for the man she thought could be Claiborne to leave. Twenty minutes later, she watched him and a deputy hold up a very shaky Eddie Calto and walk him to a waiting car. Another deputy came out with Eddie's bag and handed it to the man, who shook the deputy's hand and placed the bag in the backseat.

Julianna followed the car as it sped toward New Orleans. She watched as it pulled over in front of a private home in an exclusive part of the city. She passed a mailbox by the driveway leading to the house with the name "Claiborne" on it. That settled it. The man talking to the sheriff was Claiborne and this was his home. She watched with tears in her eyes as the men half carried, half walked her badly damaged partner into the house.

Claiborne pointed to Eddie. "Cleon, clean up Calto and tend to his wounds. I don't want him dying on us just yet."

"Sure thing, boss." Cleon stripped off Eddie's shirt and winced as he looked at his black and blue body. *Jeez,* he thought, *that bastard of a sheriff really knocked the shit out of this guy. Well, better him than me.*

Claiborne took Eddie's bags inside, opened them up, and looked through them. He pulled out the metal box where Eddie had found the two letters. But the letter with the instructions written on it was hidden beneath the false bottom, which Eddie had replaced. Claiborne picked up the first letter and, as he read it, giggled like a little baby. So the treasure was hidden in the First St. Louis Cathedral. He had the letter of release; now all he had to do was to go to the church and claim the treasure.

He dressed in his best suit, slicked back his hair, put on his gold Rolex, and drove to the First St. Louis Cathedral. He knocked on the prior's door. A slight grey-haired man answered.

"Yes, can I help you?"

"Excuse me, but are you the prior of this church?"

"Yes, I am. How can I help you?" Claiborne smiled and

handed the prior his letter of release. The priest took it and read it, showing no emotion on his face. "What is this, señor?"

"This is a letter of release."

"Release for what? I'm afraid I do not know what you are talking about."

"I'm talking about Jean Lafitte's treasure, you dolt. That's what this letter says." Claiborne was standing outside the prior's door, becoming more frustrated by the second.

"I wish I could be of some help to you, Mr. Claiborne, but unfortunately I do not know what treasure you are talking about. You tell me Jean Lafitte's treasure is hidden somewhere in my church. Don't you think if there was a treasure here, and we knew about it… wouldn't it make sense that we would have used it to build a hospital for the poor people of New Orleans? But you can see that we haven't done any such thing. No, I cannot help you. Now, I must go." He returned the letter of release to Claiborne, who watched as the little priest stepped back inside the church and slammed the door shut behind him.

Claiborne was enraged as he walked into his home, but he simmered down when he saw that Eddie was awake. He put the letter of release on the bar in the living room. "Good. You're awake."

Through a swollen jaw and busted lips, Eddie managed to slur the question he asked Claiborne. "Did you get the treasure?"

"NO! That bastard of a priest said he knew nothing of any treasure."

Eddie hacked and coughed up some blood as he laughed at Claiborne's frustration. "Well, that's that; someone must have found the treasure if there really was one, and taken it out of the church a long time ago. Probably one of the priors, figuring that everyone was dead, so why shouldn't the church keep it."

Claiborne motioned for Cleon to remove the plastic restraints from Eddie's wrists. "My family has waited two hundred years for that treasure. Every generation has waited for one of Lafitte's relatives to come looking for it. I was sure we had it when you and your girlfriend showed up. The problem now is that I'm afraid there is no treasure, so what do I do with you?"

"Look, Claiborne, I don't hold any hard feelings against you. You did what you had to do, and so did I. I didn't like getting shot at and I have to admit that I was pretty pissed off about it, but what really got me mad was the beating I took from that chicken shit Mayberry sheriff cousin of yours. Now that *really* pissed me off. If you let me walk out of here, we'll call it a day and I won't bother you anymore. What do you say? Do we have a deal?"

Claiborne hadn't expected Calto to react in this manner and he was inclined to let him go but . . . he still wasn't sure there wasn't a treasure to be found, especially since he had the release letter. "I don't know about letting you go yet. I still have a lot of unanswered questions."

"I'm afraid I can't help you with that. You see, my whole dream has just been shattered by what you claim the priest told you. Don't forget it was me that tracked down all the clues. I was the one that had to keep dodging you and the men you sent to rob my home, and especially that guy who took shots at us in our hotel room. How do you think I feel? No. I'm done with it. Can I go now? I have to find my girl and I have a little debt I owe to the guy who did this to me."

Claiborne thought fast and nodded. "Yeah, I guess you can go. I know where to find you if I need you." Thinking that Calto would lead him to the treasure, Claiborne motioned to Cleon to get Mr. Calto's bag and his belongings. Eddie wanted to grab the letter off the bar when Claiborne turned his back, but it would be noticed so, instead, he walked boldly up to the bar, took the letter and was about to place it in his pocket.

"What are you doing with that letter?"

Eddie smiled and then he winced at the pain that elicited. "I'm gonna frame the damned thing. After all the trouble I went through in getting it, what did you think I'm gonna do with it? Go to the church and get a talking down to like you did? No, I need this to prove that I found Lafitte's letter."

Claiborne was about to refuse his request, but thought better of it. If Calto had information that Claiborne didn't have, maybe he would lead him to the treasure. Claiborne smiled. "Take the letter. It's the least I could do after all I put you through."

Eddie put the letter in the metal box and laughed again; but this time he coughed, spitting blood into his handkerchief. "Shit. It looks like I have a lot of healing to do. Look, Claiborne, I've got to stay in town while I convalesce. I'm a Catholic and I go to mass on Sundays, and I'll be going to the First St. Louis Cathedral on Sunday, so don't read anything into it, okay?"

Claiborne patted Eddie on the back. "I'm sorry we got off on the wrong foot, Mr. Calto, but from now on, you won't have any further problems with me or my men. But a word of caution. Do not go to the police and drag me into anything to do with the law. I'm an outstanding member of the New Orleans community and I don't need to be dragged into a pissing contest. Understand?"

Eddie looked Claiborne directly in the eyes. "I take care of my own problems, Mr. Claiborne. I don't need the police to do that for me. Now, you warned me and I've agreed to do as you wish, but now I'm warning you. We part not as enemies and maybe not as friends, but I've given you my word, and my word is as good as gold. Now I want your word that you will not try to harm me or my girl, either here or in New York. Can we shake hands on that?"

"I like you, Mr. Calto. I hear that you gave the sheriff's brother a real beating. From what I hear, you handled yourself like you were in Special Forces or something like that. Are you ex-military?"

"Yes I was a Navy SEAL and I served two tours in Iraq and Afghanistan. I also have a black belt in karate. Those guys didn't worry me at all. It's the sheriff who gave me the beating, and he did it while I was tied down; he couldn't even do it like a man." Then he smiled at Claiborne chillingly. "But I have a long memory, Roger, and someday he'll get his. That I can promise you." His words sent a shiver down Claiborne's spine.

Claiborne put out his hand. "Yes, we can shake on it." He knew better than to try to fight Calto. If it came down to it, he'd just have him killed.

When Eddie left, Claiborne ordered Cleon to follow him and report back with anything that seemed suspicious. Although Claiborne had no basis to doubt the priest, he didn't quite believe him either. He was hoping there still might be a treasure.

Chapter 20

Nothing could have surprised Julianna more than to see Claiborne's door open and Eddie walk out of the house under his own volition. She stepped out of her car and hid by shrubs where she couldn't be seen, and watched as Eddie walked unsteadily toward her. It seemed that it was taking him forever to make his way around the corner, but as soon as he did, she grabbed his arm. He reacted by pulling his arm away until he realized it was Julianna.

"Quick, get in the car before they see us."

Cleon, who had been following Eddie, didn't expect a car to pick him up, and he watched nervously as it pulled away and disappeared around the corner. He rushed back up the driveway, got in his car, and raced down the road in an attempt to see which direction they went. If they were heading towards the heavily populated city, he would have to turn right, but if they wanted to find a smaller, more private hotel, they would have to turn left. He decided to turn left and head away from the city because that was where Eddie and Julianna were originally found. He figured they would probably head back that way. Only Cleon guessed wrong. Eddie theorized that since he no longer had to worry about Claiborne gunning for him, he'd be better off remaining in New Orleans. There were many reasons for this, one of which was that he'd be closer to the First St. Louis Cathedral. Second, he figured that Claiborne let him leave with the letter of release because this way he could keep an eye on him and watch his every move. If Eddie made an attempt to see the prior of the church, Claiborne would know Eddie knew something he didn't.

Eddie sat down at the desk in the large suite of a different hotel than that in which they originally stayed and wrote a note on hotel stationery to the prior of the cathedral. When he was finished writing, he sealed it in a hotel envelope, then, as an extra precaution, he sealed it with a strip of scotch tape, so no one could open it out without him knowing it. Eddie told Julianna he'd return in a few minutes; he was going downstairs to see if he could find someone to take the note to the prior. He told Julianna to lock the door behind him. When he got off the elevator, he scoured the lobby looking for someone, anyone he felt he could trust to do the job he needed done. He looked for messenger boys, waiters, and finally spotted a young girl pushing a laundry cart. He rushed over to her just as she was getting into the freight elevator and got in just as the door closed. He gave the elevator a fleeting scan for a security camera, but saw none and relaxed a little.

"Excuse me, miss. I'm not making a pass at you, but what time do you get off work?"

She looked at him suspiciously. "I don't see where that is any of your business, sir."

"Look I'm tied up and can't do it myself, so I'm asking you to deliver an important letter for me. I'm willing to pay handsomely for the favor."

That got the girl's attention. "And just where would I be delivering this letter?"

"To the prior of the First St. Louis Cathedral."

The mention of a priest at the cathedral removed her fears. "How much are you willing to pay? I usually go straight home after my shift because I pay a babysitter to watch my twins while I'm at work."

"I'll give you the letter and $50 right now . . . and I'll give you another $150 when you return with the prior's answer. Do we have a deal?"

"Would you pay for my babysitter too?"

"Do this for me and I'll give you $200 when you return with the prior's answer. Believe me, you have never made an easier $250 in your life."

She pushed a button and stopped the elevator. "Quick, give me the $50 and the envelope before anyone sees us. I can't afford to lose my job over this." Eddie handed her the envelope then pulled a fifty-dollar bill from his pocket. He handed her the money along with the address to the church. "Remember, you must give this to the prior, and only to the prior. It's very important that you only hand it to him and not to any other priest. Do you understand?"

"Yes. Don't worry. I get off at 4 p.m. and I'll do it then. I'll bring you back his answer and then you'll give me another $200, right?"

"Right. Don't worry about the money. I promised you I'd give it to you and I will. You have my word on that."

"Mister, I don't know you from Adam, but to put my mind at ease, could you advance me another $50, just in case you renege on your promise."

Eddie laughed. "Sure! It will be your money anyway, so why not?" He pulled another $50 from his wallet and handed it to her. "I'm in the penthouse suite. One more thing. DO NOT TELL ANYONE ABOUT THIS. I'm paying you a lot of money, not just to deliver the letter, but to be quiet about it too. I could have gotten anyone to deliver this letter, but I wanted someone I felt I could trust, and you appeared to be trustworthy to me."

She blushed. She wasn't used to getting compliments from people, especially from a nice handsome man. Even though he had black and blue marks on his face, he was still very good looking.

"I don't even know your name. What is it?"

"Doris McBride, but you can call me Doris."

"Are you married, Doris?"

"No. My boyfriend left me when he found out I was pregnant. I'm raising my children all by myself, and it's really hard."

"Do this thing for me, Doris, and I'll try to make your life a little easier." Doris pushed another button and the elevator started for the next floor. Eddie got out and took the regular elevator to the penthouse. As soon as he walked through the door, Julianna rushed over to him and asked if he had found anyone to deliver the letter. Eddie smiled and explained everything in detail.

"Are you sure you can trust this girl?"

"As much as I can trust anyone. I have a good feeling about her, though. Look, she's a working single mom with two kids to support. I feel bad for her. If she does what I want her to do, and it all works out, I'd like to reward her; you know, try to make her life a little easier."

Four o'clock came and went and they ordered room service and ate an early dinner. When they finished their meal, Eddie made drinks. At 6:22, the doorbell rang and Eddie jumped up to answer it. Doris was standing there with a blank look on her face. Eddie's heart sank. "What happened? Did anything go wrong?"

Doris's blank look vanished and a smile replaced it. "No, everything went just as you said it would. I met the prior and gave him your letter. He read it and then he wrote a note to you and sealed it in an envelope. Here it is."

Eddie thanked her and handed her $200 instead of the $150 he had promised her. Then, he asked her to write down her name and address, because some time in the future he planned on doing something nice for her. She handed him her information, but she had that blank look on her face again. Eddie followed her gaze and realized she was staring at Julianna. Doris caught Eddie looking at her and she said in a quiet voice, "She's very pretty, isn't she?" Eddie thought he understood why she had the blank look on her face. He guessed she thought she might have had a chance of hooking him but, when she saw how beautiful Julianna was, she knew she didn't stand a chance in hell.

Chapter 21

As soon as Doris left, Eddie tore open the envelope and read the note.

Dear Mr. Calto,

As you requested, I will call you on your cell phone at exactly 7 p.m. tonight to arrange a convenient time to meet with you. I do not trust the hotel phone lines. You never can tell who is listening in on them. I look forward to speaking with you later tonight.

Father Peter Benvienudo
Prior of 1st St. Louis Cathedral

Julianna was confused. "What was that note all about?"

"Look, if we're being watched, and I think we are, then we can't go to see the prior; and since we can't go to him, I figured it would work in our favor to have the prior come to us."

At 7 p.m. sharp, Eddie's cell phone rang and he picked up on the first ring. "Eddie Calto here."

"Mr. Calto, this is Father Peter Benvienudo Prior of the First St. Louis Cathedral. I'm calling as you requested. You mentioned in your note a certain party that handed me a letter."

Eddie cut him off. "Father, I'd much prefer talking to you in person, but I can't come to you. You see, the person who brought you the letter of release kidnapped me and took the letter I had searched for and found. I will answer your three questions when you get here, even though it isn't a full moon. Could you meet me in my hotel, Room 501, which is the penthouse, at, say, nine tonight? I promise you it will be a most memorable meeting."

The prior's curiosity was aroused and he agreed to the meeting.

There was a knock on the door at nine o'clock and Eddie opened it. Father Benvienudo stood in the open door, wondering what he was getting himself into.

Julianna brought the priest a cup of coffee, with cream and sugar on a tray. "Would you care for a cookie or a donut, Father?"

"No, the coffee is fine." He put a teaspoon of sugar and poured cream in his coffee and then took a sip. "I find that coffee is so uplifting, don't you agree?" He took another sip, then put the coffee on the tray and looked directly at Eddie. "What do you have to tell me, Mr. Calto?"

"For one thing, this is the wrong day of the month to visit you. I know I should have waited until tomorrow when the moon is full, but, as you can see, I was forced to come to you a day early."

"I understand, and I am ready to make an exception," the priest said. "Now, are you ready to answer my questions, Mr. Calto?"

"Yes. Go ahead and ask them."

"Where you are coming from?"

"From the west, traveling to the east."

The little priest looked at Eddie with anticipation, as if the great adventure was about to finally come to an end. "Why are you traveling to the east?"

"In order to gain more knowledge and enlightenment."

The priest smiled. "Good! Good! Now one more question please, and we are finished with this part. Are you worthy of this great honor that you are about to receive?"

"I am. I have taken a sacred vow never to abuse this great honor under the penalty of death."

Father Benvienudo pulled a handkerchief from his breast pocket and wiped his brow. "Excuse me, but may I have a drink of water?"

"Sure, Father, but I think maybe you could use a stiffer drink. How about a rum and Coke? Or a gin and tonic?"

"Yes. Maybe a gin and tonic would soothe my nerves a bit. Mr. Calto, I never dreamed this day would come. Ever since that day in August, in the year 1814, each prior of the First St. Louis Cathedral has passed on the instructions given to the first pastor of the church. And we have been passing the secret to each successive pastor, hoping that this special day would come. But it never did . . . until now. This secret has never been passed on to any of our priests, so if anyone was to come to them and ask them questions, they would have no idea what they were talking about."

Eddie interrupted the priest. "Father Benvienudo, I prayed you would see through the man who came to you today with the stolen letter. Deep down I knew you wouldn't respond to his questions."

"You needn't have worried, my son. When he came on the wrong day of the month, there was nothing he could say or do that would convince me that he was the one qualified to receive Lafitte's bequeathal. You'll need to come to the cathedral and meet with me, and I will take you to where Lafitte's legacy has rested for two hundred years."

"That's going to be a problem, Father. I'm being watched twenty-four-seven by Claiborne and his henchmen."

"Did they do that to you, my son?" the priest asked, pointing to his face.

"No, Father. But they tried to kill us in our hotel room, shooting out our windows and missing us by inches. No, this was done by a sheriff, a cousin of Claiborne, who tied my hands and beat me unmercifully. But, as you can see, I'm still alive and in the fight. But it still presents me with a problem."

The priest tented his fingers beneath his chin in thought. "Here's what I suggest. I will send three of my priests to you. They will have with them an extra set of priest's clothing, which you will put on. One of the priests will remain here until you return. When you return, he will leave with the other two priests while you remain here. It will be as if you never left your room."

Eddie beamed. "That's a wonderful idea, Father."

Father Benvienudo chuckled. "We have a priest who used to be a makeup artist when he was in films. I will make sure he is one of the three priests. He will make you up and, when you leave this room, no one will recognize you."

"Are you going to be all right going back to the church, Father?"

"Yes. I have a brother priest waiting for me in the lobby. We'll take a cab back. Besides, there's nothing suspicious about two priests meeting a friend in a hotel."

"Good. I'm looking forward to the conclusion of our great adventure, Father. Hopefully, it will be tomorrow."

The priest said his goodbyes to Eddie and Julianna and returned to his church.

Chapter 22

Father Benvienudo gave the three priests their instructions. Two of them were young, but the third was an older man who came to the church late in life. His name was Father Jacobi Vincenti and, when he was younger, he worked for the Barnum and Bailey Circus. His life changed for the better when the vice president of Disney took his young son to see the circus and noticed the incredible make-up worn by the clowns and other performers. When the show ended, he introduced himself to one of the vendors and asked who their make-up artist was. The vendor was impressed by the card, the Disney name and the man's title. The vendor called a guard over and asked him to take this man and his son to Vincent the make-up man. Vincent's real name was Vincenti, but the management of the circus had shortened it to Vincent to make it appear more American. Since then he was always called Vincent.

Vincent was busy removing make-up from the various entertainers, using jars of cold cream. When he saw the guard escorting a man and his son toward his workstation, he stopped what he was doing. "Did you want to see me?"

"Yes," the man said, and handed Vincent a fancy business card with DISNEY embossed in gold.

"What can I do for you?" Vincent was confused.

"It's not what you can do for *me*," the man said. "It's what *I* can do for *you*. I can see that you're busy, but when you get a moment, please give me a call. If you're interested, I may have a position for you."

Vincent raised an eyebrow. "A job? For me?"

"Yes. Call me tomorrow and we'll discuss it."

The following day, Vincent called the Vice President of Disney, James L. Steinberg, which was the name on the card. Shortly after that, he quit his job and worked for Disney for the next twenty-five years. Vincent was a bit over six feet tall with a solid build. He had a full head of black curly hair just starting to turn gray. He was a man alone and had always been alone, with no family or wife to come home to. Now that he was getting old, he found his family—the church, where he was welcomed with open arms by Father Peter Benvienudo.

Father Benvienudo called the three priests into his office and chuckled when he told them they were being sent on a special assignment that included playing a little deception on someone. The priests were devoted acolytes who loved their prior. He was a fair man and kind to all, and they accepted their assignment dutifully. And although they were curious, they asked no questions.

The priests knocked on the door to the penthouse at the agreed-upon time and Eddie let them in. When they left the hotel and stepped into the waiting cab, Eddie was just another priest wearing a priest's black clothing and white collar, with a large black hat that covered his face.

Cleon watched the three priests get into a cab. Cleon's accomplice, Rene, asked, "Do you want to follow them?"

"Nah! They didn't stay long. Probably had some breakfast. No, it's Calto. He's the one we're interested in."

"Yeah, but Mr. Claiborne told us to call him if anything suspicious happened."

"Are you crazy? What's suspicious about them? I'm not gonna call him for every little thing. Look, don't mention this to him because he sees a conspiracy lurking behind every door. I don't know why he wants us to follow this Calto guy, but let's not make our job any harder by calling him for every stupid thing we see."

Rene sat back in his seat. "Yeah, I guess you're right."

Eddie glanced occasionally through the back window of the cab, being careful not to arouse the driver's curiosity. He was relieved to see no one following them. The cab pulled up in front of the large church and Eddie paid the man. The cab driver was pleased to have performed this service for three nice young men of the cloth. He promised himself he would take his wife and children to church this Sunday.

When they entered the church, they intended to go to Father Benvienudo's office, but they noticed him kneeling in prayer by the altar in front of the sacristy. He stood as they approached and greeted them with a reassuring smile. "Ahh, I see that everything went as planned. There were no problems?"

"No," Eddie answered. "Everything went smoothly."

The prior released his priests. "I'm pleased with the work you have done in bringing Mr. Calto to the church as instructed. There are reasons why he had to be brought here in this manner. Soon, I will be at liberty to explain everything to you, and I promise you will find it very interesting. You two may go now. But remember, Mr. Calto will need your help to return to his hotel. I'll call you when it's time." He waited for the two priests to leave before motioning to Eddie. "Come with me. I want to show you what has been hidden here in our church for two centuries."

The little priest locked the door and pointed to a corner of the church. "That part is the old church. There were actually three churches on this site. The first was a crude wooden structure built in 1718, but a larger brick church was started in 1725 and completed in 1727. But in 1788, on Good Friday of all days, the church burnt down in the great fire of New Orleans. In 1789, the cornerstone for the new church was laid and the church was completed in 1794. I mention all this to you because it's the area near the cornerstone that we are interested in. You see, Lafitte wanted to leave a mark to show the receiver of his treasure where it was located. Come over here. We are now in the older portion of the church. Look at the stones that cover the floor and tell me what you see."

Eddie studied the flagstones covering the floor, but didn't immediately notice anything unusual about them. Then he spotted it. The stone in the corner had the square and compass carved into it. "That's where Lafitte hid the treasure?"

The priest smiled. "It's been lying under this stone for two hundred years. Every prior has been told about it, but no one has been privileged to unearth it until me. Come; I have some tools in the closet in the back. I hid them yesterday in preparation for today. I'm excited. Before we start, promise me you'll allow me to share this special moment with you. Together, we'll see for the first time in two hundred years what Jean Lafitte has hidden in here."

Eddie patted the priest on the back. "Father, if anyone deserves to see it with me, it's you. Put your mind at ease and let's get this treasure out of the ground."

They fetched the tools from the closet. Eddie picked up a crowbar. "I would really like to loosen this stone without damaging it, so let's go easy with it." He chipped away the mortar that held the stone in place and when the seam around the stone was clear, he placed the crowbar under the stone and pushed down on it. To his surprise, the stone groaned but lifted a little, just enough for him to see how thick it was. It appeared to be a solid two inches thick. He struggled with little success to lift it. Every time he managed to get it to where he might be able to wedge his crowbar under it, it slipped from his grip and slammed shut. "Do you happen to have another crowbar, Father?"

"I'll check in our tool shed." A short while later, the prior came rushing back into the church, panting, waiting to catch his breath before talking. "I couldn't find another crowbar, but I found this. I hope it helps." The priest handed Eddie a solid steel cylindrical bar. "This bar is part of an old fence."

"I think this will do the trick, Father. Let's give it a try. When I lift the stone, see if you can shove the bar into the open space." Eddie pushed down on the crowbar and the stone lifted just enough for the priest to wedge the bar under it. "Good. Now I'm going to try to move the stone slowly to the side. Just make sure the bar doesn't move, or the stone could fall back into its slot." After much struggling and sweating, the stone was moved aside, far enough to where Eddie could see a large metal chest lying in the cavity below. One end of the chest was hidden under the adjacent stone. Eddie could see the handle on the end of the chest facing him. He figured that if he could jimmy the chest on its end, it would slide out without having to remove the other stone. It was worth a try, so he reached in, grabbed the handle and pulled the chest up toward him until it was standing on its end. The chest was heavy, but manageable. "Father, give me a hand with this. It's on an awkward angle and I can't pull the chest all the way out by myself."

The priest kneeled beside Eddie and grabbed a part of the handle and together they pulled until finally the chest slid closer to the opening. "Okay, Father, I think I can handle this by myself now." Eddie pulled up and, slowly, the chest, approximately the same size as the opening, slid from its tomb with a scraping sound that reverberated throughout the large room. Before opening the large chest he lit a match and looked into the darkness below. He was surprised to see two additional chests hidden under the stones. He reached in and pulled one box through the open space. Then the second.

Once the chests were completely out and resting on the floor, Eddie pushed the stone back into place. This was much easier than getting it out. It fell into place with a heavy thud and aligned itself perfectly with the surrounding stones. Tomorrow, Father Benvienudo would have one of the priests put mortar around the great stone so it would appear the same as the others.

Chapter 23

The chests were heavy, so both Eddie and Father Benvienudo struggled as they carried them one at a time to the priest's office. They placed them on the floor and the prior locked the door and closed the blinds so no one could see what they were doing. Eddie examined the heavy nineteenth century lock on the larger chest and hit it with the hefty hammer the priest had given him, but the lock didn't budge. He decided just to cut it off. Eddie asked the priest to see if he could find a hacksaw. The Prior returned shortly with two hacksaws, one a heavy-duty commercial hacksaw. Eddie used this to cut through the top part of the lock. "Are you ready, Father?"

The priest knelt beside Eddie, his heart beating rapidly and his eyes wide with anticipation. "Go ahead, Eddie," the priest urged. "Open the chest. The suspense is killing me."

Eddie struggled with the cover of the chest, which hadn't been opened in two hundred years. It groaned and squeaked and resisted until finally giving up and opening. "These hinges could use a spot of oil," Eddie said jokingly. "What do we have here?" he said, staring at a blue velvet cloth covering the contents of the chest. He removed the cover and found packages of bound papers.

"May I?" asked Father Benvienudo.

"Be my guest, Father."

The priest removed the binding from one packet and read the individual parchments. "Oh my God. Dear Lord. These are the original deeds to the homes, land, and business properties in and around New Orleans. Jean Lafitte used these deeds to finance the War of 1812. I'm not a lawyer, but these deeds pre-date all the current deeds. Whoever owns these deeds, might own New Orleans."

Eddie whistled. "Whew! That sure is exciting if it's true. No wonder Claiborne wanted the treasure; his ancestor, the original Governor of Louisiana and Lafitte's sworn enemy, must have known about these deeds. Governor Claiborne left this information to his heirs with instructions to watch for anyone who came to New Orleans searching for Lafitte's treasure."

Meanwhile, the priest, while looking through all the old deeds, suddenly found one which made him gasp. "My God. This is the original deed to this church." The priest went to place it back with the others, but Eddie pushed his hand away.

"You keep the deed, Father. Who knows? If these deeds prove to be legitimate and legal, this deed will be good for your church."

Eddie then proceeded to examine the first of the other two smaller chests. "I can't wait to see what's in here!" The box had no lock; instead, a rod with a handle attached slid one way or the other. Sliding it to the right freed the cover and allowed the box to be opened. The mechanism worked smoothly. Inside, hundreds of gold coins filled the box to the brim. "No wonder the box was so heavy. Let's see what's in the other one." This box was a little larger but not quite as heavy. The same type of mechanism secured the cover to the body of the box. He opened it and gasped at the jewels and jewelry which filled it, probably the plunder of many Spanish ships. He studied a beautiful broach inlaid with precious stones. Then he spotted a ring fit for a princess and knew that his princess would be the one to wear this baby. "Come on; let's put all this stuff back and hide the chests." Eddie stood still, trying to figure out his next move. Then he had a flash of insight. "Father, I'd like you to do me a favor and buy me a car. I'll give you a debit card to pay the dealership. After I finish everything and tie up some loose ends, I'll come back and do something nice for you and your church. You have my word on that, Father."

The little priest wiped his brow again with his hanky then he wiped a tear from his eye. "I'm getting too old and too sentimental for this. I don't think my old heart can take much more excitement. Seeing this treasure, Eddie, has made everything worthwhile. Now let's discuss buying this car. What kind of car would you like?"

"A fast one with enough trunk space to store the treasure. Tell you what. Bring me your phone book. I'll find a local BMW dealer and have him bring the car and papers here. This way, I don't have to inconvenience you. I can take care of everything from here."

Eddie located the nearest BMW dealer and asked for a salesman.

"Hello, New Orleans BMW, Bud here. How can I help you?"

"Hi, I'm Mr. Calto. I'm looking for a new loaded BMW 7 Series car. Do you have any in stock?"

"Sure, Mr. Calto, we have plenty. When can you come in to see me?"

"That's just it. I can't come in to see you. I need you to bring the car and the paperwork to me."

"And just where would I be delivering the car, Mr. Calto?"

"I'm at the First St. Louis Cathedral. Ask for Father Benvienudo. He'll bring you to me."

Hearing that he was calling from a church, Bud thought maybe this Mr. Calto might be for real. He grew excited at the prospect of closing an unexpected high-end deal. "Uh, Mr. Calto. You do realize this is a very expensive car?"

"How expensive?"

Here goes the deal, down the drain, Bud thought. "About ninety-five thousand dollars, give or take a few thousand."

"That sounds about right to me, Bud. When can you bring it around?"

"Yessssss!!" Bud pumped his fist into the air. "I can be there with the car and papers sometime this afternoon."

"Do you have a black one?"

"Yes, I do, and it's loaded."

"Good. I'll see you this afternoon."

"I can't give you a specific time, Mr. Calto. The car has to be checked out and detailed. I'll also need some information from you. Fax me your license and insurance; and you'll have to sign some papers for the registration. I hope your credit is good, because I'll also have to organize financing."

"Don't worry about the financing. I'll pay for the car in full when you get here."

Wow, Bud thought. *I can't believe this is happening to me.* "Fax that information to me and make a $1000 deposit via PayPal. I'll hold the car and put a rush on it. I promise you'll have the car today."

Eddie was still in his priest's clothing when Father Benvienudo brought Bud into his office. He was surprised to see that "Mr. Calto" was a priest. Eddie noticed Bud staring at him. "I just came into a rather large inheritance and this car was like an itch that needed to be scratched. I could never afford it before, but now I'm scratching that itch. Now where are the papers you want me to sign?"

With the papers signed, Eddie gave Bud a check. Bud handed him the title, tags, and registration, and finally handed him the keys. Leaving the church, Bud couldn't believe his luck. This priest didn't haggle to get the price down, he didn't ask for any extras—and he paid cash. Maybe his luck was finally changing.

Eddie pulled the car around to the rear entrance of the church then he and the priest hurriedly put the treasure in the trunk. "Father, I'll drive in the back entrance of the hotel's parking garage and park there. Your two priests can come up with me to the apartment to get Father Vincent, and then take a cab back here to the church."

"Good. That will work, and no one will be the wiser."

"I'll be staying in New Orleans for a while," Eddie said wistfully. "I still have some unfinished business to attend to."

"And I can guess what that is, can't I?" the little priest replied.

"Don't trouble yourself with that, Father. No one will die."

"But don't you see, my son. I've become fond of you and I wouldn't want anything to happen to you."

"Like I said, Padre. I owe someone payback. But don't worry. I'll be fine."

"Go on now before I insist on hearing your confession." The priest slapped Eddie affectionately on the back. Eddie chuckled as the little priest went to fetch the two young priests to drive back with him to his hotel.

Eddie avoided the front entrance to the parking garage and drove around to the rear entrance. He parked on the top level. The three men took the elevator to the penthouse, where Father Vincent was watching the World Cup soccer playoffs. Eddie thanked the men, and gave them some advice.

"Don't use the front entrance. I'll call the front desk and have them bring a cab around to the back. I don't want the men who are watching me to see you leave again after seeing you leave earlier today. That might make them suspicious. You have no idea how important this favor was for Father Benvienudo and me. When you get back to the church, I'll wager Father Benvienudo will have quite a story to tell, one that couldn't be told for two hundred years. You'll find it hard to believe."

The three priests exchanged confused looks, as Eddie called the front desk. They waited for the call back to say that the cab was waiting at the rear of the hotel.

"Okay. Now do me a favor and call me when you arrive at the church. Just to put my mind at ease."

Vincent took out his cell phone. "I'll call you straight away."

"Thanks, Father Vincent. Good luck, boys." Eddie handed Father Vincent a fifty-dollar bill. "That's for the cab." Vincent smiled and thanked him.

Chapter 24

"Well, what happened?" Julianna asked excitedly.

Eddie gave her a tight-lipped smile. "Before I tell you, I have a surprise for you."

Julianna's eyes lit up. "Really? What is it? Come on now—don't keep me in suspense."

"I brought you this." And he pulled the ring from his pocket and put it on her finger.

"Oh, Eddie. It's simply magnificent. Where did you buy it?"

Then he caught himself, realizing the room could be bugged. "Step out on the balcony with me for a minute." When they were safely on the balcony, he whispered to her, "I don't know if the rooms are bugged, but I'm not taking any chances. But you, my dear, are a very rich woman."

Her eyes opened wide. "You found the treasure, didn't you?"

"Yep. And that ring is part of it. When I saw it, I knew it had to be yours. It's beautiful, isn't it?"

"It's the most beautiful ring I ever saw. Thanks for thinking of me, Eddie."

"I'm always thinking of you, Julianna. You're my girl now and I'm deeply in love with you."

Julianna looked down and when Eddie lifted her chin with his finger, he noticed she was crying. "Why are you crying? This is a time to be happy."

"I know. It's just that I'm so happy. I never thought I would ever meet a wonderful guy like you."

Eddie laughed. "I'll never understand women. You cry when you're happy. What do you do when you're sad?

Laugh?"

Under a cloudless sky with the sun low on the horizon, Eddie spent the better part of an hour giving Julianna a blow-by-blow description of everything that had transpired, up to and including his buying a new BMW. He became serious for a moment. "Here's what I figure we should do. I think we should drive to New York, deposit the treasure in a bank, and let a month or two pass. This will give me time to heal and plan my next moves."

"I don't understand. What do you mean 'plan your next moves?' It's over, Eddie. We have the treasure—and we're still alive. There are no other moves to plan."

Eddie shrugged his shoulders and shook his head. "You don't understand. Claiborne will be coming after us. He let me go because he figured I'd lead him to the treasure. I think it was his idea to have his cousin the sheriff work me over the way he did. Claiborne, it seems, doesn't like to get his hands dirty. He has other people do it for him. I didn't realize just how powerful he is in this state. It seems every other person we meet is a relative of his. So I have to figure a way to neutralize him . . . and I think I know just how to do it."

"I forgot about Claiborne. You're right. He's like a pit bull; he'll never stop looking for the treasure."

"But that's only one part of what I want to do. I still have to take care of Father Benvienudo for all the help he's given me; and then there's Doris, the girl who took the note to the padre. She could have lost her job doing that favor for me. She's a single mom with two kids to take care of. She deserves a break in life and I'd like to do something nice for her."

Julianna stroked Eddie's cheek. "That's one of the reasons I love you, Eddie. You care about other people. Of course we should do something for them. Without their help we could have never have found Lafitte's treasure. Whatever you intend to do for them, count me in. I'm with you all the way."

"Thanks, Julianna. I knew you'd say that. But there's one other little matter to take care of."

Julianna had a bad feeling and lifted an eyebrow in anticipation. "And what exactly is this one little matter you have to take care of? Because it sounds to me like we just about covered everything ."

Eddie really didn't want to tell her, but they had been honest with each other up to now. He needed to level with her. "All right, Julianna, if you insist on knowing. The little matter I spoke of is the sheriff. I still owe him some payback."

Julianna's eyes suddenly narrowed with fear. "Eddie, please. You can't be serious; you'll wind up in jail."

"Not the way I'm gonna do it. Don't worry; it won't take long. Besides, he has it coming to him."

Julianna nodded in understanding. "Let's go back inside. I could use a gin and tonic."

While Eddie went to the bar to make the drinks Julianna sat on the comfortable living room sofa. Eddie handed her a drink and took a sip of his own. "Look, Julianna, I just spelled out what needs to be done. Once I scratch these items off the list it'll be over, and we can live the rest of our lives knowing we did the right thing. We don't have to live looking over our shoulders. There will be no one left to come after us."

"Except the sheriff."

Eddie waved his hand to make light of her comment. "Forget about the sheriff; he won't even know who did it to him. Don't underestimate me, Julianna. I've survived much worse situations than this little squabble with the sheriff. Now, the only question is . . . would you rather remain in New York—or return with me to New Orleans?"

Julianna put her arms around him. "I know you'll have to come back here. Do you think that now that I've fallen in love with you I'd let you come to New Orleans by yourself? I'm with you until the end."

"If you agree, here's what I'd like to do. We'll stay here for tonight. I'll call the front desk and ask them to give us a wake-up call at 5 a.m. We'll have a quick breakfast then get in our car and drive to New York."

Julianna smiled. "It sounds like a plan to me."

"Good! Then let's pack our bags before we hit the sack, so we don't have to do it in the morning."

Eddie fired up his MacBook Pro and did a Google search for the best way to get from New Orleans to New York. "According to Google, the trip north is twenty hours and forty-eight minutes, taking US Route 11. I'll just plug our address into the BMW's GPS and have either Ramona or Carlos take us home."

"Who are Ramona and Carlos?"

"I haven't checked out the voice on the GPS yet. If it's a female's voice, it's Ramona; if it's a guy's voice, it's Carlos."

The following morning, Eddie put their luggage in the car, but they found the dining room closed. "Come on; we'll drive a couple of hours then grab a bite to eat on the road."

Driving home in the luxurious BMW was a joy. The car ate up the road quickly and the fatigue factor didn't enter into the equation. The ride home took two days. There was no rush, and they decided to stay overnight in Virginia.

Chapter 25

Julianna jumped out of the car, unlocked the front door, and held it open to make it easier for Eddie to take in the luggage. "Let's get inside and heat up a pot of coffee."

"That sounds good."

Eddie was surprised to find two men waiting for him inside. One was a security guard from the firm he hired to watch the house, and the other was a uniformed police officer. Eddie was confused. Something was obviously wrong.

The guard stood and introduced himself. "Hi, I'm Tommy Ricco. While you were gone," he explained, "a guy broke into your home. He was shot and killed by August Day, the man on duty at the time. During the altercation, Day was also shot. We would have called you, but you left instructions not to call, so we handled it ourselves."

"You did the right thing. If you'd called there was nothing I could have done but come home, and that wouldn't have solved anything. Now tell me about the man who was shot. Is he gonna be all right?"

"Yeah, he's recovering nicely; he'll be all right."

Eddie turned to the cop. "I know why he's here, but what are you doing here?"

The cop introduced himself. "I'm Officer Walsh, part of a three-man shift ordered to wait here until you returned. My boss wants to have a few words with you. I'll call Detective Lieutenant McGovern to let him know you're back."

Officer Walsh left the room briefly to make the call.

"Okay, he's on his way. Stick around and don't go anywhere."

The security guard spoke up. "Well, now that you're back,

Mr. Calto, I'm leaving. I have to file a report."

"Thanks, Tommy. Tell your boss I really appreciate the job you guys did."

Tommy smiled. It was nice to be appreciated. "Thanks, Mr. Calto. I'll be sure to tell him that.'

About an hour later, McGovern walked in. "So, you've finally decided to come home, eh?"

McGovern's remark rankled Eddie. He became defensive and looked the detective in the eye.

"Look, Detective. How long I decide to stay on vacation is my business and none of yours. In fact, we almost decided to remain in New Orleans for another month. Now I understand you have some questions for me. Let's get them over with. I'm tired from the trip home and I don't need to be talked down to by a goddamned cop."

The detective realized he had got off on the wrong foot. He had to reestablish some sort of rapport with Eddie. "Look, I didn't mean it the way it sounded. It's just that I have to talk to you and the wait was killing me. What do you say we start over again?"

Eddie relented. He was tired and had a short fuse. He had let it get away from him. "Tell you what. I'll put on a pot of coffee then we'll sit down and you can ask me all the questions you like. Is that a deal?"

McGovern smiled and put out his hand. Eddie took it. "A cup of coffee sounds real good right about now."

"Fire away, Lieutenant."

McGovern pulled a card from his shirt pocket and handed it to Eddie. "Do you know this man?"

Eddie looked at the card and raised his eyebrows. "Where the hell did you get this card?"

McGovern smiled inwardly. Maybe now he'd have a lead. "This was found in the wallet of the man who was killed after he broke in here. Do you know this man?"

"I sure do. He's the guy that tried to have me killed. He, or one of his men, took a shot at us while we were in our hotel room. We were lucky to get away alive. That's one of the reasons we left New Orleans."

"*One* of the reasons? What are the other reasons?"

"Lieutenant, I'll make a deal with you. I'll tell you everything right from the start and when I'm finished, I want your promise that you'll help me get this bastard."

McGovern shook his head. "No can do, Eddie. I have to know what you want me to help you with. I'm not promising anything until I know all the facts. If—and it's a big if—if I believe you need my help, I may agree, but not until you tell me everything. So, why don't you start from the beginning?"

Eddie spent the next two hours explaining everything to McGovern. How he was initially contacted by a high-priced lawyer who arranged a meeting. And how, at that meeting, Eddie was given a chest left at the firm by his great-great-grandfather. He described to the detective the clue that was left in that chest, omitting for the moment the gold coins and the jewels.

Then Julianna told her part of the story. How she was related to Jean Lafitte's brother, Pierre, and what she discovered in Pierre's diary. About how she first came to meet Eddie. She explained why they decided to travel to New Orleans together to find Lafitte's treasure.

Eddie described in detail how the sheriff arrested him and beat him to within an inch of his life. The detective winced as Eddie described the beating. Eddie's face was still black and blue. He told McGovern how Claiborne kidnapped him and only let him go because he figured Eddie would lead him to the treasure. "He'll be coming after me and Julianna. He'll send his henchmen to get us. He must know by now that we have discovered something. He feels it should be his."

"What exactly did you discover?"

Eddie turned to get the pot of coffee. His eyes locked with Julianna's and he gave an almost imperceptible shake of his head. His eyes warned her not to say anything. "You want to know what we found, right?"

"Yes."

So Eddie explained how Lafitte collected all the deeds from all the property owners in New Orleans to finance the War of 1812.

"Deeds? That's the treasure you found?"

"Don't turn your nose up at those deeds. I'm going to have my lawyer check to see if they are still relevant. If they are, Julianna and I will own New Orleans."

McGovern whistled. "I never thought of that. Whew, no wonder Claiborne wants the treasure. He's a big landowner in that section of Louisiana and you would own everything he owns. In fact, you'd become his landlord. No wonder he's gunning for you. He probably knew all along what you were looking for, although you had no idea."

Eddie didn't tell him about the jewels and the gold coins. Now was not the time; besides, it was none of his business. "Well, you heard our story. Now, will you help us? You know he'll be coming after us, and I'd like to plan a little trap for him. But I can't do it without your help."

McGovern's eyes widened and he smiled broadly. "Go on. Explain your plan. This is getting interesting."

"When he comes for me, I'd like to somehow trap him with his own words. Maybe we could set up some sort of surveillance system to record our conversation."

"That's doable. I can have our tech support team set up a surveillance system in the house. What worries me is when you're not home. I'll assign a team to follow you wherever you go. My men are pros and even you won't know you're being followed. I don't want this guy to slip away from me again."

"Again?" Eddie said.

"Yeah. I went down to New Orleans and spoke to him. He's a slick bastard, I'll give him that much. He told me a fairytale about the guy that tried to break into your home. I didn't buy it for a minute, but I had nothing to go on until now. Now I'll get him." The detective took some pictures from his pocket. "Do you recognize the man in this picture? I took a long shot with my iPhone so the picture isn't very clear, but maybe you recognize the guy."

Eddie picked up the pictures and gave a slight nod then handed the pictures to Julianna.

"Does this guy look familiar to you?"

"Yes he does." Eddie handed the pictures back to the cop. "He's one of Claiborne's hired goons."

The detective gave a curt nod. "I figured as much. Look, I'm heading back to the precinct, but I'm assigning an unmarked car to watch your house. I'll give you a call tomorrow morning around nine. If anything comes up in the meantime, I'll either call you or come here." The two men shook hands. Before McGovern left, he again apologized to Eddie for mouthing off at him earlier.

Eddie called his lawyer and, although the attorney was in a conference, he took the time to answer Eddie's question. "Tom, I need some advice. What I need to know is this. If everyone in New Orleans gave Jean Lafitte the deed to their property to use as collateral to finance the War of 1812, and those deeds were hidden away somewhere and discovered two hundred years later, would they still be relevant today? Would they supersede all deeds that followed? If they are valid deeds, would the person in possession of them theoretically own New Orleans? Is that a workable hypothesis?"

"That sounds plausible, Mr. Calto. The Indian tribes in

different parts of the country are currently asserting these types of ownership claims. Be honest with me, Mr. Calto, was that a hypothetical question, or did you or someone you know actually discover those deeds?"

"We did indeed discover those deeds, Tom, through a lot of hard work. We had to unravel a number of clues which ultimately led us to Lafitte's treasure, namely the deeds."

"Wow, this is gonna be one hell of a case. It's sure to make headlines around the world. Just let me know when you're ready to proceed. I'll take a look at the deeds and have an expert check their authenticity and validity. Then we'll test their plausibility in court."

Chapter 26

Claiborne paced the room, puffing on his long, Cuban cigar, the smoke drifting upwards in billowing white clouds toward the ceiling. This was something he never permitted himself or anyone else to do—smoke in his house. But today was different. Today, he was aggravated and mad as hell, furious because he felt that Eddie Calto had somehow pulled the wool over his eyes. He kept reassessing what had transpired and came to one conclusion. Calto must have found the treasure and, once he had it, left town—otherwise he would still be here. He couldn't prove that Calto had found the treasure but in his gut he knew he was right. He would make an example of Edward Calto and he'd take back what was rightfully his. "Go home and pack a suitcase, men, because we're flying to New York tomorrow morning."

The next day, three men boarded an early American flight to LaGuardia Airport. Arriving in New York in the early afternoon, they booked rooms at the LaGuardia Airport Howard Johnson motel. After settling in, they went down to the lounge area and took a table near a window, far enough away from any guests to discuss their plans without being overheard. "How do you want to handle this, boss?"

"We've got to be careful, after that policeman came all the way from Queens to New Orleans to question me because of that fool Joe Morte. I don't think he suspects that I had anything to do with Morte, but I don't want him to know I'm in New York. That would give him a reason to tie me to Morte and Calto. I don't want to be surprised the way Morte was when he broke into Calto's home and found himself staring at an armed security guard. The best thing is to wait for Calto to leave his house and grab him on the street."

Tim, one of Claiborne's men, asked, "What if he has that girl with him? You know, the one he brought with him to New Orleans?"

Claiborne acknowledged the question. "She'll be with him, all right. It seems the two of them have become joined at the hip. Well, we have no choice but to grab the two of them. I hope I'm not put into the position of having to terminate one or both of them. I find that distasteful and unnecessary. But if I have no other choice, it will be entirely their fault."

Gerard had been silent up to now."I don't think we should grab them on the street, boss," he said. "Too many people could see us. I think we should spend a few bucks and send them some flowers. Only I'll be the guy delivering them. This way, I can see who's there and who isn't. If no one is protecting them, we can just go in there and take what we want."

"That's absolutely brilliant, Gerry. That's what we'll do. We'll buy some flowers and sign the card in the detective's name."

* * *

Eddie had telephoned the security firm he originally used and told them he would like a two-man detail to be at his home tomorrow morning to take some very important papers to his lawyer in Manhattan.

A squad of policemen was waiting in Eddie's house for instructions from McGovern. Before he spoke, Eddie gave the security guards their instructions. "Take this box to Mr. Thomas Carruthers of Epstein, Harris & Berg in the Times Square Tower at 7 Times Square in Manhattan. Give to him and no one else, understand? The address is on the box."

"Anything else before we leave, Mr. Calto?"

"Yes, I want you to remain at the lawyer's office. When I tell Claiborne the deeds are there, I believe he'll attempt to steal them. Be careful. Nothing is worth your lives, especially two hundred-year-old pieces of paper. Claiborne will kill for what's in that box."

McGovern warned them. "This box had better make it to the lawyers in one piece. I'm holding you both responsible for getting it there, so be on your toes and don't take this assignment lightly."

Eddie winced, hearing McGovern speak to the men like that. Jake Morgan, one of the guards, looked at McGovern. "You may be a cop, McGovern, but we're just as professional as you are. You don't have to tell us how to do our job, and you don't have act like you expect us to take off with whatever's in this box. For your information, I don't give a rat's ass what's in this box or what you have to say. We'll do our job and this box will get to the lawyers. If we have to, we'll die guarding it. Do you understand where I'm coming from? The trouble with you, Lieutenant, is you think everyone you meet is a crook. Well, for your information, some of us take our jobs seriously. Now, if you don't mind, step aside and we'll be on our way."

"That's telling him, Jake," his partner Murray chimed in.

Lieutenant McGovern stood with his mouth open, but couldn't think of a thing to say, so he turned and bellowed at his men.

"I thought you'd like to know," Lieutenant McGovern said loudly enough to get everyone's attention, "a party of three, consisting of Claiborne and two of his men left New Orleans this morning on an American Airlines flight to LaGuardia airport. They landed a half hour ago and they booked rooms at the Howard Johnson Airport motel. If I were to take an educated guess, I'd say you're about to have some unwelcome visitors." He turned his attention to Eddie. "These men didn't come to New York just to kill time seeing the sights. They came here for one purpose, to get those deeds. I'm staying here with you. These men will be stationed near the house, disguised as homeless people, sanitation workers, or a mailman. They'll be close by if we need them." McGovern turned to his men. "You have your instructions. Be on your toes. One man has been killed and a private detective wounded, so we know these men are desperate and dangerous. If it comes down to you or them, take them out and we'll worry about the left wing, lily-livered politicians when the time comes. You all have pictures of Claiborne, and airport security gave me pictures of his two men." McGovern handed out the photos. "You all know what to do, so get out of here and catch me some bad guys."

Eddie pulled McGovern aside. "In a moment I'm going to make a phone call and I want you to know exactly what I've done."

McGovern's face tightened and he ground his teeth. "You're not going to do something stupid, now, are you?"

Eddie gave him a tight-lipped smile. "No, nothing stupid. I don't want to see anyone getting hurt, so I'm going to call the two security guards at the law office and tell one of them to sit behind the desk and pretend he's my attorney. Claiborne's men won't be expecting that."

McGovern smiled, showing a set of yellow, tobacco-stained teeth. "Sounds like a good idea to me."

The smile remained on McGovern's face. But as he walked out the door, he muttered words that sounded something like, "Shit—now civilians are running the show."

Chapter 27

The leased black Mercedes pulled near the curb and parked on the other side of the school. Tim got out, holding a bouquet of flowers. He walked through the schoolyard, crossed 42nd Street, stepped up to the door and knocked. When Eddie answered the man handed him the flowers. "Special delivery. You have to sign the receipt, but I seem to have left my pen in the truck. Can I come in and use one of your pens?"

Eddie smiled disarmingly. "Sure; come on in."

Tim stepped into the house and took a quick glance around—and Eddie caught him doing it. "Were you expecting someone else?" he asked.

Tim realized he had been caught looking and tried joking his way out of it. "No. I was just admiring your house."

"Oh? What exactly is it about my house that you admire?"

"Well, it's a big house and I can see you live alone. That's all I meant."

"Oh, I see. The fact that I live alone makes this house seem better. Right?"

"No, I didn't mean it that way." Tim was getting nervous. He was anxious to get out of there. "Look, as much as I'd like to stay and chat I have other deliveries to make. Sign by the X."

Eddie signed and Tim handed him the copy. Tim left in a hurry, crossed the street and rushed through the schoolyard to the waiting Mercedes. A postal worker, sitting in his truck, busy sorting packages, spotted Tim get into the open back door of the black Mercedes. He watched as the car sped away and disappeared around the corner, but not before the postal worker wrote down the tag number and a description of the man. Earlier, as he sorted his mail, he had jotted down descriptions of the two men waiting in the car. He started his truck, drove around the block to Calto's home, and went into the house.

"Did you get the license number, Mel?" asked Eddie.

"Yes, and I called it in. It's an Avis rental car issued to a Gerard Tucker from New Orleans."

"Okay, then. Now we know for sure that Claiborne is here and has two men with him. My guess is that we're going to be getting company in the next few minutes. You better get back to your postal truck and make believe you're delivering letters." The undercover cop left, sorting the letters, just as a black Mercedes pulled up in front of the house. Mel kept walking in the direction of the next house, where he placed a blank envelope in the mailbox. Then he walked to his truck, pulled it up past the next few houses and began the same routine, putting blank envelopes in mailboxes while keeping his eye on the men who stepped out of their car.

Claiborne, with his two men following, walked up to Eddie's house and knocked on the door. Eddie answered with a surprised look on his face. "Why Roger, what are you doing here?"

Claiborne looked past Eddie to be sure no one was with him. He couldn't see anyone, which put him at ease. "Do you mind if we come in? There are a few things I'd like to discuss with you."

"To be honest with you, Roger, I don't mind you coming in, but I'd like your friends to remain outside, if you don't mind."

"But I do mind. Normally, I wouldn't care, but what I have to discuss with you would include them. So if it's all right with you, we'll all come in for, let's say, a cup of coffee."

Eddie wanted to aggravate Roger so he'd show his true colors and reveal the real reason for his visit. "Sorry, I want your two friends to stay outside while we have our little discussion."

Claiborne, suddenly and without warning, pushed Eddie forcefully with both his hands. Eddie wasn't expecting it and stumbled as he fell backwards, but caught himself and remained on his feet. Claiborne and his two goons walked in and closed the door behind them. "Is anyone else here?"

"No. Why?"

"Your girlfriend. Where is she?"

"She's at her motel. Why? What the hell is going on here, and what do you want to talk to me about?"

Claiborne's eyes flared angrily. "What do I want to talk to you about? Is that what you're asking me?" But before Eddie could say anything, Claiborne answered the question. "I want to talk to you about the treasure you found. I know you found it, so there's no sense lying about it. Where are the deeds?"

Eddie smiled for the first time since Claiborne and his men entered his house. "So you know about the deeds, eh?"

"Yes. My ancestor knew Lafitte buried them somewhere; he just didn't know where. For two hundred years, we Claibornes have been waiting for someone like you to lead us to them. The deeds belong to the Claibornes and no stranger has a right to them. Now, where are they?"

"Sorry, but you're too late; the deeds are at my attorney's office."

McGovern was listening to every word, but he needed to nab Claiborne in the act of actually stealing the deeds. He could arrest him now for harassment and bodily harm and a number of other charges, but he'd be out on bail before the ink on his arrest warrant was dry. McGovern slipped out the back door and radioed his men, giving them instructions to rush to the law firm of Epstein, Harris & Berg. He told them to remain in disguise. "Have one of the men dress like a window cleaner or a janitor. I want someone close to Calto when they attempt to leave with the deeds." After completing his call, McGovern slipped quietly back into the house through the back door and put on his headphones so he could listen to what was being said.

"Get your jacket, because we're leaving," said Claiborne. As Eddie was putting on his jacket, he asked Claiborne, "Why do you want those deeds so badly? You know you're not going to get away with this. Too many people will see you. They'll recognize you when the police show them your picture."

"SHUT UP! Just shut up. I must have those deeds. My family has been waiting for them to surface for two hundred years and now that they've been found, it's up to me to retrieve them. THE DEEDS ARE BY RIGHTS MINE, and no one else's. Can't you get that through that thick skull of yours? The spirits of my ancestors are watching me even now, because those deeds belong to us Claibornes, and my ancestors want them back in our possession."

Eddie could tell by Claiborne's ranting that he was insane. He'd have to tone down his words when speaking to him. "You have the address. Why do you need me to go with you? If you want the deeds so badly, go and get them. They've caused me nothing but trouble ever since I found them."

Claiborne smiled malevolently. "You are coming with us, and once those deeds are in my possession, I'll deal with you myself. Come on, men. Take him with us—and see that he doesn't get away."

Chapter 28

McGovern was concerned that something could go wrong and someone could get hurt, so he made a quick telephone call to Eddie's attorney, Thomas Carruthers, and identified himself to his secretary as a policeman. He told her it was urgent that he speak to Mr. Carruthers. The secretary quickly got Carruthers on the phone. "Mr. Carruthers?"

"Good morning, Detective McGovern. What can I do for you?"

"Did the deeds arrive safely?"

"Yes, I received the deeds and the two men who brought them are still here in the outer office. What's the problem, Detective?"

"Claiborne and his two men have taken Eddie Calto hostage and are using him as leverage to get the deeds. They should be arriving at your office shortly. These men are dangerous, so when they ask you for the deeds, give them to them, and don't worry about the repercussions. I assure you, we know all about their plans. My men will be waiting outside and, when they leave the building, they'll be arrested and taken into custody. In the meantime, do as Calto suggested and have one of the men who brought you the deeds sit behind your desk and pretend he's you until the threat has passed. Now put one of them on the phone, please. I'd like to speak with him."

A minute later, a voice said, "This is Jake."

"Jake, this is Detective McGovern."

"Yes, Detective. What's up?"

"Listen, Jake. I want you to sit behind Carruthers' desk and be him until these men leave. I don't want him getting hurt. My guess is that Claiborne won't want to be involved in taking the deeds. He'll want plausible deniability. If I know him, he'll prefer to remain away from the action and out of harm's way. I could be wrong, but I'm getting to know the man, and from what I've learned, he's a behind-the-scenes kind of guy. No, he'll let his henchmen take the chances and do the dirty work and, if they're caught, he'll deny sending them up there for the deeds."

"No problem, Detective. That's what Mr. Calto is paying us for."

"Look, Jake, I don't want Eddie getting hurt, but don't take any chances with the other two guys. Have your gun handy and if they reach for their guns, don't hesitate. Take them out, but don't hit Calto, understand?"

"Don't worry, Detective, both Murray and I are ex-NYPD and we know how to handle ourselves."

"Christ, why didn't you guys tell me you were ex-NYPD. I feel like a damn fool now."

"Ahh, forget about it, McGovern; we all make mistakes every once in a while."

As soon as McGovern hung up with the security guards he called the team leader of the men he sent to the law firm. "Gil, it's McGovern. Okay, the guards that Eddie Calto hired are going to pretend to be lawyers. Jake will be your contact and he'll sit behind Carruthers' desk and be him as long as the bad guys are there. I told him to give them the deeds but, if they went for their guns, they were to take them out. But as far as you and your team are concerned, remember Eddie Calto is a hostage and I want him safe; and I'd like to have one of the perps alive so he can confirm it was Claiborne that put them up to robbery."

"Don't worry; we'll be careful and if these guys make it out of the building, we'll make sure one of them lives. I'll give

Jake a call right now and tell him we're positioned outside."

"Do you have all of the exits covered?" McGovern asked.

"Jesus Christ, Yancy, do you think this is the first rodeo I've been to? Of course I have all the exits covered. Look, you do what you have to do, and let me do my job, which, by the way, I'm very good at."

Although the man couldn't see him, McGovern shrugged his shoulders. The man was right. "Sorry about that, Gil, I forgot what a good cop you are."

"Aww, forget about it, Yancy. Look, I'll call Jake and tell him we're ready out here." Gil hung up and called Jake. "Jake, it's Detective Gil Estrello. We're all set up and ready to go."

"Got it, Gil. We'll keep in touch. We'll take care of the situation here. Don't worry about Calto—and I promise one of those two bozos will still be alive when this is over."

Claiborne pulled into the parking garage near the lawyers' building in mid-Manhattan and ordered his two men to go get the deeds and take Calto with them. The three men approached the receptionist.

"Can I help you?"

"Yes. We'd like to have a word with Mr. Carruthers," Gerard said politely, with a phony smile plastered on his face.

"Mr. Carruthers is busy at the moment. Do you gentlemen have an appointment?"

"No, this is a private matter concerning Mr. Calto. It won't take but a moment. I'd appreciate it if you'd call him and ask him for a minute of his time."

The receptionist looked at the men suspiciously and then at Eddie, trying to decide if she should or shouldn't call him. She couldn't read anything on Eddie's face, so she dutifully picked up the phone and buzzed Mr. Carruthers' office. "Mr. Carruthers, Mr. Calto is here to see you with two gentlemen. I told them you were busy, but they are quite insistent. They said they will take just a moment of your time." She nodded at the telephone. "Mr. Carruthers will see you now. His office is the third door on the left." As soon as Carruthers hung up the phone, he slipped into the adjoining office and Jake took his place behind his desk.

The men entered Carruthers' office and looked cautiously around, but the only men in the room were the two security guards, one acting as Carruthers and the other apparently busy with a file. Gerard and Tim looked around for an old chest before approaching the desk, but there was no sign of it. Instead, a large cardboard box lay in a corner by the window. Jake sat behind the desk while Murray stood by his side, holding the file. "You gentlemen wanted to see me?" asked Jake.

"Yes. We did."

"What can I help you with?"

Tim just came out with it. "We want the deeds that Eddie Calto sent here this morning. Are they in that box over in the corner?"

"Why, yes, they are."

"We're taking them with us. No one will get hurt unless you try to stop us."

"We have security in the building. You'll never get away with it."

"Yes we will." They pulled out their guns. "Now, both of you back up against the wall." Murray turned to put the file on the desk but, as he turned, he grabbed the gun hidden under the manila folder. In a practiced move, his arm flashed upward, pointing the gun toward the two men. At almost the same instant, Jake grabbed the gun hidden on his lap by the desk and, before Claiborne's men realized it, they were in trouble. Tim dove behind a plush chair, but he was too late. As he dove, Jake shot him in the back. As he fell lifelessly to the floor with a heavy thud, Eddie's training kicked in and he dropped to the floor and scurried towards the wall away from the gunshots.

"Get your hands up, unless you want more of the same." Jake waved his gun at Gerard. "Check to see if he's got a second gun." Murray found a thirty-two snub nose Colt in a holster on his ankle." Then Jake picked up his cell phone and called downstairs to McGovern. "One dead, one alive, and Calto is fine. Come on up and take this piece of shit out of this office."

A short time later, McGovern sat Gerard down in a chair while the coroner took Tim away in a body bag. "Who sent you for the deeds? Was it Claiborne?"

"I'm not saying anything. I want a lawyer," Gerard said without conviction.

McGovern toyed with Gerard like a cat playing with a mouse. "We have Claiborne in custody," he lied. "He said he knew nothing about what you two had planned. He said he just accompanied you here and waited while you took care of some personal business. He acted shocked when we told him that two men he knew had attempted to steal some worthless deeds from a heavily secured law office. He denied knowing anything about what you two morons were doing up here." With a hint of a smile, McGovern looked directly into Gerard's eyes and told him in a low voice, "He's gonna lay you out to dry, baby, and you're gonna do twenty years hard time while he'll be outside, free as a bird."

While Gerard was Claiborne's muscle, he didn't want to take the fall for his boss's hare-brained scheme. He only went along with him because he was being paid very well. He wasn't about to go to jail if he could help it, and he wasn't about to take the rap for his boss's stupidity. He was getting nervous. At first, he figured Claiborne would hire a lawyer and pay his bail, but now he had the feeling that wasn't going to happen. He looked up at McGovern. "If I tell you what you want to know, what do I get out of it?"

"It's not you I want; it's Claiborne. If you help me, I'll help you. I'll reduce the charges and make sure you make bail. But that's only if you give me what I want; otherwise I'll pin everything on you, and you know I have the evidence to make it happen."

"Okay, okay, I get it. Let's get started. Ask me your questions." When Gerard finished talking, Claiborne was as good as convicted. Now all McGovern had to do was to arrest him and book him.

Chapter 29

The two policemen assigned to monitor Claiborne watched as he waited nervously for his two men to walk out of the building with the box of deeds. But so far, neither had been seen leaving the building. He began to worry. They'd been in there too long. He took out his cell phone and called Gerard. To his surprise, Lieutenant McGovern answered. "Yes."

Claiborne, not realizing it wasn't Gerard, asked, "Did everything go all right?"

"No, it didn't, Claiborne."

"Hey, wait a minute. Who is this?"

"This is Detective McGovern. I'm sorry to tell you this, but one of your men is dead and the other is in custody."

Claiborne acted surprised. "Oh my God, what did they do?"

"You can cut the act, Claiborne. Your man Tucker told us everything. I'm afraid you'll have to come with us." Claiborne quickly hit END on the phone. He intended to get in his car right then and leave, but when he turned around, he was surprised to see two NYPD policemen standing there.

"Turn around and put your hands on the car." Claiborne did as the police requested and, while his hands were on the car, the police patted him down. "Put your hands behind your back." They handcuffed him and put him in the backseat of the squad car. One of the officers spoke into his radio. "We have Claiborne cuffed and in the squad car, Lieutenant."

"Good work, men. I'll be right down to collect him."

The squad car was driven to the front of the Times Square Tower. Claiborne remained in the backseat while the two cops got out to talk to McGovern.

Eddie tapped McGovern on the shoulder. "Yeah, what is it, Eddie?"

"I have to go upstairs and talk to my lawyer for a few minutes. Could you have one of your men take me back to my house when I'm done?"

"Sure." He pointed to a cop. "Paddy, put Claiborne in my car and wait here for Calto. Then take him back home, okay?" It was an order not a request, and the cop knew it.

"Sure, Lieutenant. We'll be waiting here for him."

"Good." Just then, the two security guards walked out of the building and McGovern called out to them. "Hey, guys. Come on over here for a minute. I just wanted to apologize for mouthing off before; and I wanted to tell you that you did a great job up there."

While the two guards and McGovern talked, Eddie took the elevator to his lawyer's floor. He walked to the open door and knocked on it, and his lawyer waved him in. He wore a thin smile on his face, coupled with a look of relief, now that the excitement was over. "Did the police get Claiborne?" he asked.

"Yes. He's sitting in the back of a police car, waiting to be taken to the 110th Precinct, where he'll be booked."

Eddie was on pins and needles over the deeds, anxious to know more about them, so he changed the subject. "How far did you get with the deeds, Mr. Carruthers? I'm curious to know how you would begin to process deeds that are two hundred years old. Do you intend to approach the city of New Orleans, or maybe go through the courts? Or will you try to deal directly with the individuals occupying the properties mentioned on the deeds?"

Carruthers tried to answer Eddie in layman's terms. "I'll have to go to New Orleans, and then to the county or town where the property is located and search to find out whether the deeds were ever recorded two hundred years ago. If they were recorded, then we'll have to file a lawsuit to enforce the deeds. On the other hand, if the deeds were not recorded, we may be out of luck, because the general rule is: 'first recorded' is first in right. However, we'll be able to file a lawsuit to challenge the other filed deeds. Let me research the deeds and the laws in the counties that pertain to them and I'll get back to you with my recommendation."

Eddie wasn't through yet. He still had one important question for the lawyer. "In your opinion, do you think Julianna and I will ever get any money from the deeds?"

Carruthers sat back in his plush leather chair and steepled his fingers beneath his chin. "If all the deeds were found to be valid by the courts, those deeds could be worth twenty or thirty billion dollars or more. And even if just some of the deeds are valid, you'll still be in a position to receive a substantial amount of money; however, it may be a tough battle because the various landowners would probably tie you up in court for years, rather than agree to pay you one dollar. I would thus think a generous negotiated settlement would be the best solution for the concerned parties."

Eddie left the building a much happier man. It appeared that Julianna and he would wind up wealthy, and maybe even stinking wealthy. *Boy, wouldn't that be nice*, he thought to himself.

"Ready, Mr. Calto?" one of the cops asked.

"Yep, I'm ready. Thanks for waiting for me."

Now that the danger was over and Eddie was home, he called Julianna on her cell phone and assured her it was safe to return to the house.

"I can't wait to see you. There's such a lot to tell you."

Chapter 30

While Eddie was waiting for Julianna, he locked all the doors in the house as a precaution. When the house was secure, he went down into the basement and pulled the drain grating aside to gain access to the hidden safe. He opened the safe, pulled Lafitte's plundered jewels out and laid them on the large worktable he had set up in his basement. Then he began sorting the rings, bracelets, and necklaces into separate piles in order to make it easy to find a particular type of jewelry. While sorting through the rings he came across an exquisite ring that he pulled aside to give to Julianna. When all the jewelry was sorted and put into its proper grouping, he placed each group of jewels into a separate canvas bag. He wound up with four large canvas bags, which he then placed neatly into the box and returned to his hidden safe. Then he went upstairs, put up a fresh pot of Dunkin Donuts coffee, and sat at the kitchen table waiting for the girl he intended to marry to come home.

The two lovers talked small talk over coffee until Eddie surprised her and took her hand in his. "I have something important to ask you, Julianna, and it can't wait."

A surprised look appeared on her face and her heart beat quickened in anticipation of the question she hoped he would ask. "What is it, Eddie?" she stammered.

There was no stammering in Eddie's reply. "I want to marry you. I want you to be my wife. I went out with a lot of women in my life, but I never felt towards any of them the way I feel towards you. What do you say? Do you accept my proposal of marriage? If you say yes, then you have to put this ring on your finger."

Eddie took the ring from his pocket and put it on her finger. The diamond had to be at least three carats, with rubies on either side of it.

"Oh, Eddie, this is the most beautiful ring I've ever seen."

"I was sorting out Lafitte's jewelry when I came across it. It's even nicer than the other ring I gave you; and I thought what a nice engagement ring it would make, and how nice it would look on your finger."

Tears of happiness glistened in Julianna's eyes. "I'd almost given up waiting for the right man to come along and ask me to marry him; but when I first met you, I felt something for you I've never felt for any other man. And that first night when we made love, it was an absolutely magical experience. Yes, Eddie, I would be honored to be your wife. And I accept this ring as my engagement ring. I can't wait to show it to my mother and to all my friends."

Eddie looked pensive.

"What's wrong, my love?" Julianna asked.

"Well, I still have a few loose ends to tie up. I have to go back to New Orleans and I'd love you to come with me. If you say yes, then the only question is, do you want to go before or after we're married?"

"I'll go whenever you want."

Eddie thought about it for a minute. "Let's see if I can narrow this down a bit. Julianna, do you want to have a large wedding or just a small church ceremony with a few close friends? It's up to you."

"Well," she began thoughtfully. "Every girl wants a church wedding and to wear a beautiful white gown with her father walking her down the aisle." It saddened her that her father was no longer alive, and that this could never happen. She pulled herself together and continued, "I'd like to have pictures of our wedding to show our children. And if we have a daughter, I'd like her to wear my gown at her wedding."

Eddie nodded. "That settles it, then. I'm going to have to wait for our lawyer to get back from New Orleans. That might take a while with so many deeds. So while we're waiting, we're going to have us a church wedding with a very large reception, serving the best food money can buy."

The date was set and the wedding would take place in three months. The invitations had been printed and mailed. Eddie invited most of his buddies from the firehouse, plus some firefighters from a few other firehouses. The ceremony was to be held in St. Leo's Catholic Church and reservations were made for the reception at Riccardo's Restaurant and Catering House in Astoria, Queens. Over the months, Julianna got to know Captain Schieda, Eddie's former boss, very well, and she asked him to walk her down the aisle in place of her deceased father. Julianna was surprised when she saw the priest who would marry them. Eddie gave Father Benvienudo an all-expenses paid vacation to New York just to officiate at their wedding ceremony. This delighted the priest. He was honored that Eddie thought enough of him to invite him to New York to marry them. In fact, Father Benvienudo was the talk of the wedding among the guests. The story of the successful Lafitte treasure hunt had been leaked to the internet and the media by Eddie's high-priced lawyer. Everyone in the country knew of Jean Lafitte's pirate treasure, and the role the little priest had played in recovering it.

Thanks mainly to the electric celebrity atmosphere that pervaded their upcoming wedding, when the day finally arrived it was a rousing success. Newspaper reporters, cable news trucks, and even Drudge himself, were there to get a story. Unlike some celebrities, Eddie was generous with his time, and both he and Julianna gave the media what they wanted: plenty of pictures and a Cinderella story that made front-page news and kept the cable news outlets busy for weeks. Because Julianna was a beautiful woman and Eddie a handsome man, they looked as though they had stepped out of a romantic movie. Eventually, Eddie signaled time out. "I think you fellas have enough information, so if you'll excuse us, we still have guests to greet at our reception in the next room. If any of you haven't eaten yet, tell the headwaiter and he'll take care of you; and remember that the bar is open all night, so don't be afraid to ask for whatever you drink. I don't want to see any of you media people leaving my wedding sober, you hear." The media loved him and they didn't intend to let him down. Eddie smiled warmly, then both he and Julianna left to resume their places on the dais.

After the wedding when all the guests had left, Julianna and Eddie returned to their home in Corona. They had planned to delay their honeymoon until they heard from their attorney concerning the deeds. If everything went as planned, they'd get into their new BMW 7 Series sedan and take off for their honeymoon in New Orleans.

Two weeks passed and, finally, Eddie received some news. "Mr. Calto, it's Tom Carruthers. I just got back from New Orleans and I have some good news for you. Most of the deeds had been filed two hundred years ago when the property was originally purchased. Our law firm will take the matter through the courts and I believe the outcome will be extremely favorable to you. I'll get back to you when I have some more information."

When he hung up the phone, Eddie looked at Julianna. "Pack up your bags, honey. We're leaving for our honeymoon right now."

Riding in the big BMW was like sitting in a cloud as it ate up the miles with a smoothness and comfort that made the trip down south not at all tiring. They weren't in any rush, so every four or five hundred miles, they pulled off the highway and spent the night at the best hotel they could find. In the past, Eddie used worry about every dime he spent. He'd have to count his pennies to save enough money to travel somewhere. It was strange how fate worked. One day he was broke and the next everything had changed. He could go where he wanted, and stop where he wanted. He could eat the best foods without worrying about the bill of fare. Life was good, and he intended to shower his new wife with luxuries they had never dreamed of. It was like living in a dream, and they had to soak up all the pleasures before the dream ended. Only this wasn't a dream. It sure was nice not having to worry about money any longer. God bless their ancestors, he thought. If it wasn't for his great-great-grandfather remodeling Lafitte's old blacksmith shop, the old man would have never found the clue and the chest with the jewels. And Julianna, being a direct descendant of Pierre Lafitte and finding his diary in her great-great-great-grandfather's sea chest. It appeared to Eddie that the universe was magic in the truest sense. It caused their lives to unfold in such a way that they had to meet, fall in love and, together, find Jean Lafitte's pirate treasure. He found solace in the belief that Julianna and he were soul mates, destined to meet.

Chapter 31

Julianna and Eddie enjoyed the ambiance of the honeymoon suite in the Ritz-Carlton. They also enjoyed their lavish meals in the third-floor lobby in the Davenport Lounge, which took its name from their headline entertainer, Jeremy Davenport. The following day, they stopped at the First and Second St. Louis Cemeteries, where they visited the graves of Pierre Lafitte and Dominique Youx; but they had no luck finding Jean Lafitte's grave. They inquired with a tour guide, who informed them that there were suspicions that Jean Lafitte, like Elvis, had faked his own death and retired to a farm somewhere and lived to a ripe old age.

Back at the hotel, Eddie sat Julianna down on a comfortable chair in the Davenport lounge to have a few words with her.

"Julianna, it's time for me to take care of the few loose ends I told you about. I'd like to discuss them with you now." Julianna knew this was something important to Eddie so she waited to hear what he had to say. "I'd like to take care of that young lady who helped me when I needed help. You know, the girl who took the note to Father Benvienudo. Then I'd like your permission to give Lafitte's jewels to Father Benvienudo to display in his church." Julianna started to speak, but Eddie put up his hand. "What I'd like us to do is select certain pieces of jewelry to keep in our vault and then either give or lend, whichever you prefer, the rest of the jewels to him. I owe him much. Without his help, we would have none of this, and I feel he deserves something. Attendance at his church has dropped significantly since war was declared on the Catholic Church and on Christians in general. By displaying the jewels in his church, he could increase attendance tenfold. Now, if you object to this, I'm open to suggestions; but one way or another, I have to pay my debt to him."

"Let's loan the jewels to him, Eddie. We worked so hard to find them and we went through such hardships, it seems a shame to just give them away."

Eddie smiled at her. "You're right. We did work hard to get them and we went through hell to keep them. All right, let's loan the jewels to him. In fact, I have a suggestion that should make him happy."

"What about the girl? What do you want to do for her?"

"Well, she's a single mom who's working her butt off to feed and clothe her children. I'd like to buy her a new car and a small home and put a few bucks in her bank account. Besides, she's part of what I have planned for the padre."

"Can we afford to do this for her?"

"Sweetheart, we're going to be billionaires. Besides, I have over a million dollars cash that I inherited from my ancestor. Don't worry about money. We have plenty of it with a lot more coming in."

Her eyes were wide and she took a deep breath. Eddie was right. "Besides," Eddie added, interrupting her thoughts, "there's still the little matter of my fire department pension. No matter what happens to us, I'll always receive a small monthly check and that alone would tide us over."

Julianna smiled briefly. "All right. That takes care of the priest and the girl, was there anything else?"

Eddie nodded and his eyes narrowed. This next part was hardest for him. Julianna was his wife now, and he wasn't going to start their life together by lying to her. So he was honest. "I still have to take care of the sheriff."

Julianna's eyes widened in fear and she put her hand to her mouth. "Eddie, no. Don't do it. Don't be crazy; just let it go."

He smiled patiently at her. "Julianna, this man almost beat me to death. He had me strapped down where I couldn't defend myself and beat me to within an inch of my life. I can't let him get away with that. He's gotta be taught a lesson and I'm just the guy to teach it to him. Tomorrow, I want you to go on a shopping spree. Buy whatever you like and don't worry about me. I'll be back sometime during the night."

Julianna wanted to stop him, but she knew she was married to a real man who would resent her if she interfered now. This was something he had to do, but that didn't mean she wouldn't worry herself sick until he returned and she could hold him in her arms again. "All right. Do what you have to do, but don't kill him, and don't you get yourself killed, understand?"

"I understand, baby, and don't you worry. When these three matters are taken care of, you and I are going on a luxurious trip around the world."

The next day before he left, Eddie checked his glove compartment to make sure his black ski mask and his Sig Sauer 230 were still in his glove compartment. He drove away, pointing the car north, in the direction of the sheriff's jurisdiction.

Eddie wore a Paul & Shark reversible red and black jacket with the collar pulled up around his neck. He wore it on the black side so he would blend in with the darkness later in the evening. A New Orleans Saints cap and Prada dark sunglasses made him practically unrecognizable. He sat in his car and waited patiently most of the late morning and early afternoon. He was determined to stay in town long enough to pay the sheriff back. He had all the patience in the world. He knew that sooner or later the big oaf of a sheriff would come walking out the jail and get in his car, thinking he was as safe as in his momma's womb. Eddie didn't care whether he walked or drove; the end result would be the same. Eddie's demeanor had changed. He had taken on the persona of his combat days. Combat was scary, but what he was about to do here was a piece of cake. He didn't have to worry about snipers, car bombs, grenades, or handheld RPGs firing rockets at him; all he had to worry about was getting one small town panty-assed sheriff alone somewhere, and letting the man know what it felt like to be on the shitty end of the stick. So he waited . . . He waited patiently. It was 7:15 and getting dark. Glancing at his watch, he almost missed the sheriff walking down the ramp, about to turn into the parking lot. Christ! He started his car as the sheriff got into his car and took off in the direction away from town. Eddie kept on his tail, but not close enough for the sheriff to know he was being followed. Eddie followed the car down a dark two-lane road that was badly in need of resurfacing. The sheriff pulled off into the dirt parking lot of an old roadhouse that looked as if it had last been painted forty years ago. There were three cars parked in the front, close to the entrance. The sheriff parked alongside the last of these, got out of his car, and swaggered into the roadhouse as if he owned it. About twenty minutes later, the front door opened and the sheriff walked out, wiping his chin with his jacket sleeve. He stood there for a moment and counted out some bills, then laughed, put the bills in his pocket and headed toward his car. As he opened his door he felt metal pressed against his spine. A hand reached around and took his gun from its holster and a voice asked, "Are you wearing an ankle gun?"

"No."

"If I search you and find you have one, I'm going to hurt you real bad. I'll ask you again, are you packing any other heat?"

The sheriff nodded, reached down and pulled a small, cold snub nose 32 from his ankle holster.

"Careful now. Don't do anything foolish. Now, hand me the gun by its handle and get in the car." The sheriff got in his car and Eddie climbed in the passenger's seat. "Now drive down the road until we find a nice quiet place where we can talk."

The sheriff turned to look at the man holding the gun, but Eddie stopped him. "Keep your eyes on the road. Don't look at me."

The sheriff glanced at his face but saw only the ski mask. "Look, I don't know what you want, but kidnapping an officer of the law could get you put away for a long time."

Eddie snickered. "Do I look like I'm worried about the law? Just keep driving until I tell you to stop." They drove for another five minutes, until Eddie spotted a road leading into the dense woods. "Pull onto that road and keep driving." They drove a short way into the woods and, when the squad car couldn't be seen from the road, Eddie told him, "Stop here, shut off your lights and turn off the engine. Now get out of the car." Eddie took a rope from his pocket, tied a slipknot on one end, slipped it around one of the sheriff's wrists, and yanked it tight. "Come over here by this tree and place your back against it." Eddie wound the rope around the tree, then tied the other end to the sheriff's other wrist and pulled the rope tight, leaving the sheriff no wiggle room. Satisfied that the sheriff couldn't move, Eddie reached into his back pocket for a pair of black leather gloves and put them on. "You like to beat guys when they have their hands tied, eh? Well, how about a little dose of your own medicine?" Eddie hit the sheriff with all of his might, right smack in the gut. Then he punched him hard in the face, opening up his lip. Eddie was in pretty good shape, so he hit the sheriff as if he was a punching bag until he became arm weary.

The sheriff began to plead with him. "Please . . . no more, no more. Why are you doing this to me?"

Eddie was tempted to take off his ski mask and reveal himself, but thought better of it. "Why am I doing this to you? Because you do this to other people, that's why. Now why don't you relax for a while until I catch my breath, because I'm not finished with you yet, Mr. Lawman."

The sheriff lay limp, but Eddie shook him in an attempt to revive him. Slowly, the sheriff came around. "Good. You're awake. Are you ready for dessert now?" Eddie punched him square on the nose, shattering it so that it split open like a ripe tomato. "Hey, that one was pretty good; now, let's see if I can do the same to your eyes."

The sheriff groaned. "No, please, I'll do whatever you say, but no more, no more, please. I can't take it."

"So, you can't take it, but you're pretty good at dishing it out, eh? Well, I think that's about enough for today. Before I leave, I'm going to give you a little piece of advice. If I ever hear that you tied someone else up and beat him to within an inch of his life, you won't be so lucky, 'cause I'll come back; and next time I won't be so gentle. Next time, I'll kill you."

The sheriff shuddered with fear, knowing this man would kill him without a second thought. With that said, Eddie punched him harder than ever, knocking the man cold. Eddie drove the police car back to the roadhouse and parked it in the back where it was dark and the car couldn't be seen. Then he returned to the BMW and began the hour-long drive back to his hotel, whistling "Put on A Happy Face." His car ate up the road, burning miles as he headed back to New Orleans and his new bride.

Chapter 32

The sleek black BMW pulled to the rear of the First St. Louis Cathedral and stopped. Eddie shut off the car's whisper-quiet motor and Julianna and he got out and knocked on the door to the rectory. The door opened and a surprised Father Benvienudo stood in the open doorway, gaping speechlessly at his two new friends. He quickly recovered. "Come in, come in. Please have a seat. Theresa! Theresa!" he shouted, and soon a stout middle-aged woman came hurrying into the prior's rectory.

"What is it, Father?" Then she noticed his two guests sitting at the table.

"I didn't mean to frighten you, Theresa, but would you be so kind as to put up a pot of coffee for my guests?" As Theresa went about dutifully preparing the coffee, Father Benvienudo turned to his guests. "What brings you two young people here?"

Eddie couldn't help grinning. It always made him feel good when he helped someone. In the fire department, he knew he'd done something important when he saved someone's life, or safely removed them from a dangerous situation. Well, he had that feeling now. "Now that the story about the treasure hunt has gone viral and everyone in the world has apparently heard about Lafitte's Treasure, has your attendance picked up?"

The prior nodded. "*Si*, it has picked up quite a bit, but not as much as I had hoped."

"Well, Father, I think we might have solved that problem for you."

The little priest's eyes lit up. "What do you mean, Eddie?"

Eddie looked at Julianna for a sign to proceed, which she gave with a slight tilt of her head. "Father, Julianna and I were thinking about what to do with Lafitte's Treasure and came to this conclusion. We feel it would be safer here than in our home, or in a bank vault, gathering dust. We want people to see this treasure, so we've decided to loan all the jewels to this church, except for a few items we'll keep for ourselves. Once word gets out that the Lafitte jewels are on display here, we're sure people from all over the world will come to see them. I can picture this church overflowing with curious people who want to see the treasure. But you'll need security measures brought in to safeguard the treasure. We'll cover that expense. And here's another suggestion. If you would like the church to make more money, I think you should put together a church tour to show people where the treasure was buried and how it was found. You could hire a professional writer to write a story, a dialogue if you will, describing how the clues were found and how they eventually led us to the treasure. If you incorporate a church tour along with the treasure, I know it will be successful and generate a lot of additional income for the church. Julianna and I will donate the parchments we unearthed containing the clues, so the people on the tour will get a better idea of how we discovered the treasure. Travel agencies would love it and so would the elected officials of New Orleans. Tourism would jump exponentially, with people curious to see the famous pirate's treasure."

Father Benvienudo was so excited with Eddie's suggestions that he couldn't wait to act on them.

"You'll have to find space somewhere in the church to display the jewels," Eddie continued, "and then you'd have to hire armed guards twenty-four-seven to protect them. But I promise you, your church will be overflowing with people wanting to take the tour and see the treasure."

The priest grabbed Eddie and hugged him, then Julianna. When he spoke, his eyes were glistening with tears. "I'm so happy. You two have made me so very happy; I can't thank you enough. Yes! I too can see the church overflowing with curious people, and I intend to take advantage of it. The jewels will give me a chance to spread God's word to them. I'm anxious to start. What do we do next?"

"Remember, there will also be people who want to steal these very same jewels, so before you do anything, you'll have to get insurance. I'll call Lloyds of London today."

It turned out that Lloyds knew all about the jewels and were anxious to have their name associated with them. Their United States representative, James Sperlment, would fly out to meet with Eddie tomorrow afternoon.

"Where are the jewels now, Eddie?" the priest asked.

"In the trunk of my car."

"What?" The blood drained from the priest's face. "Don't you think you should put them in a bank vault to protect them?"

"I thought about doing that, but decided against it."

"But why, Eddie?"

Eddie sighed. "I don't want anyone to know the jewels are here. If I brought them to the bank, people outside the bank would know of it. Thieves could wait until I go to the bank, either to bring the jewels in or to take them out, and figure a way to steal them. No. I'll keep them in my car for a day or two until I can bring them in here. But we can't prolong this because there's always the chance that someone could steal my car, never realizing that the precious jewels are hidden in the trunk. But put your mind at ease; I'll take care of this. First, I'll call a reliable security company and arrange to meet with one of their representatives. If we're lucky, maybe he can come here today. Meanwhile, you must figure out where to display the jewels. Pick a dramatic spot, so that when people come into your church, the jewels will jump in their faces. Word will spread quickly. But the jewels must also be in a safe spot. Not near a window or a door. I'll leave that to a good security company to figure out. Come now; let's find ourselves a security company."

Eddie called the security company he'd used in New York and found they had a branch office in Louisiana. He was given the name and number of their subsidiary, New Orleans Security Consultants. Eddie learned that one company did the installation of alarm systems while the other provided private detectives, personal security and property protection guards.

The representative arrived at the church within the hour and, after he examined the church thoroughly, he gave Father Benvienudo his recommendations. "I suggest, Father, that we build the cases for the jewels on that wall opposite the altar. By placing the display cases there, they'll be away from any windows and doors. It's open enough that a thief would be seen if he tried to break into the cases. I will install the latest alarm available with two or three fallback safety measures."

Eddie interjected his thoughts. "How soon can you install the display cases, and will the jewels be safe in them?"

The security man nodded. "Good question. Burglars like to break into a business through an adjoining wall. We'll install a large, hidden safe where the jewels will be stored at night and we'll install the jewel cases away from an outside wall and on their own pedestal, secured to an inside wall. If possible, we'll make the safe invisible. I take it you need the display cases installed yesterday?"

"That's exactly when we want them installed!"

"Okay, I'll get on the phone and see what's available. If we have any pre-built high-tech bulletproof glass cases built and in our warehouse, I'll see to it that we get them here first thing in the morning. I'm also going to have Louie LaForte, the best safe man in the business, come over and install your safes. I'll brief him on what needs to be done. He'll meet with you and give you his opinion on which safe you should use and why. Okay?"

"Very good." Eddie liked what he'd heard so far. These guys were real pros.

The next day, a team of professional security experts came to the church to install the state of the art bullet proof glass display cases. While the men were installing these, a short, thin man with a broken nose and a full head of unruly dark brown hair walked in and asked to speak to Eddie. "Are you Mr. Calto?"

"Yes, and I assume you must be Mr. LaForte. Right?"

"Yes, that's me. Is Father Benvienudo here? I'd like to speak with both of you so that I don't have to repeat myself."

"He's here. Wait a minute and I'll get him."

"Do you have someplace we can be alone, where we won't be disturbed?" LaForte asked when the priest arrived.

Father Benvienudo nodded with satisfaction. "I know just the place; please follow me. We'll go to the rectory. No one will bother us there."

LaForte was the restless type. He stood to explain what he intended to do, while Eddie and the priest sat. "First, I want to give you a little advice, and take it from an old safe cracker."

Eddie and the priest looked at one another. "Were you actually a safe cracker?" Eddie asked.

"Yep. Not only was I a safe cracker, I was the best in the business and that's why the company hired me. You two and the church will be the beneficiaries of my life of crime.

"Most times, thieves will look for a place to rent just above the place they're gonna rob. They will then cut part way through the floor, but not completely—not yet, anyway. Then, sometime early in the morning, one of the men will climb a telephone pole a couple of blocks away and will have no trouble finding which wire to cut. The phone company usually puts a tag on the line so they'll know which line is for the telephone. Once he cuts the wire, the store's alarm system will be disabled. Now, when the line is cut, the police and our alarm company will be alerted and send a team to the store. But they'll find nothing wrong because there will be no sign of a forced entry. They'll check the store and the property to see if anything is amiss and then, finding nothing, they'll call the manager or the owner at home and tell him an alarm came in, but they saw no sign of a break in. They'll suggest to the manager that he have someone stay on the premises as a precaution until Monday, when the telephone company can make repairs. But the manager will tell the police that he spoke to the alarm company and was assured that the alarm was working fine. So the manager sees no reason for anyone to remain there. Now, here's the tricky part. When the burglars see the police leave, the burglars will cut through the rest of the floor and take whatever they came to steal.

"Some very skillful burglars perform most of these crimes. They are known to the FBI as YACS. YACS is an acronym for Yugoslavia, Albania, Croatia, and Serbia. This type of crime evolved when the Soviet Union collapsed. When it did, these criminals left Russia and made their way to the United States, which became their new home. Once these professional thieves were securely entrenched here, they were anxious to test their skills against our laws. I know from firsthand experience that they are very successful. They're good at what they do, and that is breaking into and stealing from places like this. So we must be one step ahead of them. These guys are so good they're thought to be the cause of an estimated loss of over fifty million dollars.

"I'll tell you how creative they are. One of the establishments I'm familiar with had a TRTL 30X6 safe and they broke it open with the use of a special tool that was originally designed to cut through the hulls of ships sunk during the Second World War. They used an Arcair Slice Pack, which uses 'burning bars,' which are thin, hollow lengths of metal, to break into that safe. These bars get real hot and they burn at 9,000 degrees F. So compare that to steel which melts at 2,500 degrees F. This is what you're up against, Father.

"But don't worry about anything because you have me here to help you, and I promise I'll give you a system that will make those YACS wish they never attempted to rob you, if they ever tried. If you can afford it, I would suggest installing two TRTL 30X6 safes with separate combinations. At night, you'll put half the jewels in one safe and half in the other. That way, if the thieves do manage to break in here and rob one safe, you'll still have the other half in the second safe."

Father Benvienudo looked to Eddie for advice. "I think having two safes is a good idea. Install them where you think they'll be safest and hardest to get to and I'll pay for everything."

Louie looked at Eddie with newfound respect. "Good choice. I'm leaving now, but I'll be back later today with the two safes. Meanwhile, the glass enclosures are almost finished."

"Should I bring the jewels in now or wait for you to return?"

"Wait until I get back. I don't want anyone knowing the jewels are anywhere near here. Not until I get back and install the safes."

Chapter 33

It cost Eddie much more than he figured to install the safes and alarm the wired glass display cases. Eddie called Manhattan Security Consultants back to let them know that he needed security men to guard the treasure. After discussing the sort of protection the church would need, he informed them that the jewels were to be brought into the church within the next few days. Manhattan Security Consultants would provide around the clock protection. He asked that they be onsite from tomorrow. MSC would guard against anyone breaking into the glass enclosures during the day or the safes at night.

Eddie was particularly concerned for the safety of the jewels during the transfer from the glass cases to the safes at night. Father Benvienudo asked that the guards monitor the perimeter of the church while his priests made the transfer to the hidden safes. He preferred that not many people, not even the security team, know where the safes were hidden. Louie LaForte had them installed in a small, hidden nook behind the wall in the sacristy, and encapsulated them in concrete to make it more difficult for thieves to break in if the hidden room was discovered. As an added protection, the room was not just hidden; LaForte built it as if it was protecting the gold in Fort Knox. The room was a small fortress that could only be accessed by a combination of a retinal scan and thumbprint. If anything were to happen to Father Benvienudo, the security firm could access the room through a secondary combination known only to Manhattan Security Consultant's president, with the agreement of both Father Benvienudo and Eddie Calto.

Within a few days, everything was in order and it was time for Eddie to bring the jewels into the church. Two Manhattan Security Consultants armed guards met Eddie and Julianna at their hotel and accompanied them to the church, sitting in the backseat of their car.

It was a short ride to the church. There had been a lot of speculation and media coverage, so crowds gathered early, and some brave souls had camped overnight so they could be the first to see Lafitte's treasure as it was placed into the glass cages. The car pulled up behind the church and the two guards cautiously climbed out with their hands on their guns, just in case they were needed. The guards' eyes scanned the area in every direction, but all appeared normal. Four priests waited by the rear door, looking out the window, ready to dash out and help bring the jewels into the church as soon as the car arrived. Eddie pushed the trunk release button on his console, and the trunk sprung open. This was the signal for the priests to dash out and bring the jewels into the church. The guards were even suspicious of the priests, who could be thieves dressed as priests, intending to steal the treasure. Only when Father Benvienudo spoke to the guards and confirmed that they were priests in his church did the guards relax and turn their attention back to the area around them.

Since Eddie had separated the jewels into four different categories, it was easy to display them properly, placing the necklaces in one case, rings in another, and bracelets in still another. There was a separate display case for miscellaneous jewels such as diamonds, emeralds, sapphires, and rubies, which were plentiful. Once the jewels were enclosed in their cases and the alarms turned on, Father Benvienudo signaled to the priests that the doors to the church were to be opened. The throngs who had been waiting patiently to see the treasure rushed down the aisle, only to gape in awe at the beautiful selection of jewels that had been buried for two hundred years.

It had been suggested that the jewels be placed in a separate room built just for them and that the church charge a moderate entry fee. But Father Benvienudo dismissed the idea. "I will not have my parishioners pay to come into my church. These jewels are for people all over the world to see and appreciate."

Eddie suggested that a small fee would help pay for the infrastructure needed to support the display, but the little priest wouldn't consider it. The priest finally agreed to charge for the church tour, which would explain the history of where and how the jewels were found. Eddie hired a PR firm to design a professional tour package, which would include the parchments, also housed in bulletproof glass cases, with the codes that led to the clues. Eddie always had this idea in mind since he first asked the young girl to deliver a message to Father Benvienudo; so he suggested to Julianna that this would be a perfect opportunity to hire Doris to manage the tours. The church settled on a nominal fee for the Lafitte Treasure Tour, and Eddie was confident from the first day that it would be a rousing success. He was also confident that the church would be filled to capacity during mass, with people from all over the world here to see the famous Lafitte Treasure.

Eddie's job was done. The only thing to do now was inform Doris that she had a new job. Eddie and Julianna wanted to do much more for her. Satisfied that everything was in order at the church, they headed back to their hotel to relax, have dinner, and discuss what else they were going to do for Doris besides getting her this job.

Chapter 34

Eddie wanted to buy an apartment for Doris and her two sons, but Julianna disagreed. "Buying a home is a very personal thing and usually a woman knows what she wants in a home. So I think that if we're going to do that, we should have Doris come with us." Eddie couldn't argue with her logic. Since Doris worked during the day, they would go to see her that night at her home.

That evening, the black BMW pulled slowly down the seedy street, looking for the right address. They pulled up in front of a rundown apartment house. They entered the building, walked down the hallway to Doris's first floor apartment, and Eddie knocked on the door. A female voice answered from behind the door. "Yes! Who is it?"

"Doris, it's Eddie and Julianna Calto, the guy that gave you the note to bring to the priest at the cathedral. Remember?"

The door clicked open and Eddie saw the frightened look on Doris's face. "Sure, I remember you. Sorry I took so long to answer the door. I don't usually get callers at night." Doris looked around her sparse but clean apartment. "Please come into the living room. It's small, but we can sit and talk there."

"Look," Eddie said. "We're not going to take up much of your time. I told you when you helped me that I would do something nice for you, and Julianna and I figured out something we think you'll like. We want you to quit your job tomorrow. Call them in the morning and tell them you had another job offer."

"But I can't do that. I don't have any other job offer."

"Yes you do. I'm sure you've read about the Lafitte

treasure on display in the First St. Louis Cathedral. Well, Father Benvienudo needs someone to take charge of the tours the church is giving, and we all agreed that you are the person to do that. Of course, you'll be getting a raise and you'll have an assistant who will relieve you on your days off. Tomorrow, before we do anything, we'll stop and buy you a new Ford Focus; then we're going shopping for a condominium for you and your kids. You don't have to worry about the cost. This is all on Julianna and me."

Doris couldn't believe her luck. Dreams do come true. All because she helped someone in need. Eddie had said at the time that he'd do something nice for her, but she didn't believe him. People often say things when they want something from you; but even though she didn't believe him, he looked desperate. So in spite of her doubts, she decided to help him. And look what came of it. Instead of being fired, she had a new job that paid more than her old job; she left the Ford dealership driving a new Ford Focus; and now Julianna had a list of condos for her to look at. Doris was so happy she could cry. After visiting four condos, Doris chose the first one. All she had to do was sign the papers.

The last stop for the day was the Cathedral and Father Benvienudo. The little priest loved Doris immediately and she him. She would start her new job in the morning.

The firm that prepared the tour came to the church in the morning and Doris was instructed on what to wear, how to behave and, finally, what to say. Her prepared talk was written in a clear concise manner and placed in a professional presentation folder. It explained how Eddie discovered and solved each clue, starting with the one his ancestor found in the blacksmith shop

The jewels were displayed safely, Doris was taken care of, and the sheriff was out of the way. It was time to go home.

***

Julianna placed a cup of coffee in front of Eddie. "We have fresh donuts in the refrigerator; do you want one?"

"No. Not now. I was just thinking that we accomplished the three items that needed closure and now we're free." There was still one more item of importance to discuss and that was the deeds. In the morning, he'd call his lawyer and see how he was progressing. Then, perhaps, they could discuss going on a real honeymoon—maybe a trip to Europe. But Eddie didn't care where they went as long as they were together. He told Julianna to choose anywhere in the world she wanted to go and he'd take her. "Other than calling my attorney to see how he made out with the deeds, we can leave for Europe anytime you want."

The phone's shrill ringing woke Eddie from his thoughts. "Hello? Yes, this is Ed Calto. Who's calling please? . . . Oh, Detective McGovern. Good to hear from you. What's happening? What? When? Okay, I'll be on the lookout for him and thanks for the heads up."

Julianna heard every word Eddie said and didn't like the sound of it. "What happened, Eddie? What was that call about?"

He slumped back in his chair. "Every time I think we're free to go, something seems to pop up to prevent it."

"What happened?" Julianna asked nervously.

"It's Claiborne. His lawyer got a change of venue. He appeared before a friendly judge in New Orleans . . . probably another relative," Eddie added. "And the case was dismissed because of lack of evidence. His lawyer argued that Claiborne was in the car and had no knowledge of what his two associates were going to do. As far as Gerard's confession goes, Claiborne's attorney argued that the man would say anything to keep from going to prison. The judge dismissed the case and Claiborne's now free to do as he wishes. I would take an educated guess that he'll be coming here to see us."

A few minutes later, the phone rang a second time. Eddie answered the phone apprehensively. Then he physically relaxed. "Oh, hello, Father Benvienudo. What can I do for you?"

"Eddie do you know who came into the church today and took the tour?"

"Let me guess, Father. Roger Claiborne, right?"

"Yes, but how did you know?"

"I just received a call from the detective who arrested him. He told me a judge in New Orleans dismissed the charges for a lack of evidence. Don't worry about me, Father. Just make sure your security team knows that Claiborne is free and still very much a threat. Wait until he finds out we might own all of his properties. That'll really set him off. As soon as I know anything, I'll call you. Goodbye, Father."

"What did Father Benvienudo want?" Julianna asked.

"Claiborne just took the tour."

"Wow that was fast. So what do we do now?"

"I don't know. I guess we'll just have to wait and see what he does next. But one thing is certain."

"What would that be?"

"We must be very careful until he tips his hand. Hey, for all we know, he may give up his insane quest and stay in New Orleans."

Julianna laughed. "Yeah. Fat chance of that happening."

Eddie agreed. "Yeah, you're probably right, but you have to admit, it sounded pretty good."

A sad smile remained on her face. "Oh, Eddie, what are we going to do?"

"Well, we could go on our honeymoon to Europe as we planned. What do you say? Do you want to do that?"

She shook her head. "No, Eddie. How could we enjoy ourselves with Claiborne always on our minds, wondering what he's up to? I'd be afraid he would follow us to Europe and come after us without any fear of the law."

Chapter 35

Julianna buckled her seatbelt and, when the BMW with Eddie driving reached 111th Street, he made a right turn and pointed the big car toward the Long Island Expressway. As he approached the corner of 46th Avenue, he heard a loud pop and then another popping sound. Suddenly his car swerved violently to the side, almost hitting a parked car. He managed with some difficulty to pull the car parallel to the curb. He got out of the car and looked at what caused the car to swerve. Nothing was wrong on his side of the car. But on the passenger side he had two flat tires. He quickly opened the passenger door, unbuckled Julianna's seatbelt and pulled her roughly from the car. "Come on. No time to lose." He dragged her across the street and through the gate into Flushing Meadows Park.

"What happened? Where are you taking me?"

"Someone shot out the tires and we're not waiting to see who it was. We need to get out of here and fast." He led her to the area of the park that abutted the Long Island Railroad.

"Why are you taking me here? Wouldn't it be better to head for the ball fields or maybe over there in the wooded section of the park?" She pointed past the ball field to a densely wooded section where they might find a place to hide.

"No, just stay close to me and trust me. I know what I'm doing." He looked behind him and noticed two men running through the gate toward them. "Get down low."

She wondered why they stopped by some hedges, when they could have kept running. Eddie, hidden by the hedges, reached down and lifted a manhole cover. He told Julianna to climb down the ladder, and he'd follow close behind. Once she had climbed down, he pulled the cover back in place and climbed down into the darkness of the large sewer.

"Eddie, I'm frightened. It's so dark in here."

"Take out your iPhone and turn on your flashlight." Eddie did the same.

Behind her silt and soot had filled the back part of the sewer. "What do we do now?"

"Come on. The guys following us may have seen us enter the sewer and, if they did, they'll come down here after us. We have to move fast now."

"Where are we going, Eddie?"

"Trust me. I know this sewer like the back of my hand. Many years ago, during the first World's Fair, between 1939 and 1941, there was a Cowboy and Indian exhibition along the whole area we just walked over. This sewer was in service back then, and even for the second World's Fair in 1965. If we had time, I would like to try to find the underground house that's still buried here somewhere. I know all the furniture was taken out of it, but it was too expensive to remove the thick concrete walls. It's here somewhere. I remember as kids we played ball here all of the time and, when we weren't playing ball, we searched for it."

"Did you ever find it?"

"We knew the location. I don't remember what the street was called, but it was located opposite the Lowenbrau Gardens Pavilion. One day, we found a depression in the ground near that spot and we were sure that if we dug around a bit, we would find the entrance. But we never went any further because, after being buried for fifty years and because of the mold and dampness, we were afraid the air would be poisoned; you know, like King Tut and the curse of his tomb. That was nothing more than contaminated air that poisoned some of the people who first entered his tomb. Besides, this underground house, which was designed to withstand an atomic bomb, is probably full of water. This park is situated on marshy land. Even if it's not filled with water, there is probably mold on all the walls and floor."

"Maybe not," Julianna added. "If the house was designed to withstand an atomic bomb, it might have withstood the ravages of time and neglect."

"Yeah, I guess you have a point there. But right now, it won't do us any good."

"Do you know where this sewer ends?"

"Yeah. If we keep walking straight ahead, we'll come to seven steps that lead down to the waters of Flushing Bay. We'll get off at the exit before the end. That will let us out close to Shea Stadium. If we're lucky, we can hail a cab. When we get back home, I'll call Detective McGovern and tell him what happened. Then I'll call BMW and have them send someone out with two new tires and drive the car home. But right now, we have to keep going. The way this sewer twists and turns, I don't know if we're still being followed."

"I can't wait to get out of here. This place is spooky."

"Yeah, I know. Just make sure you keep to the sides while walking. There's still some water flowing down the center of the tunnel." They finally arrived at the exit Eddie was looking for. "Wait down here while I shove the manhole cover aside, then climb on out of here."

Julianna shuddered. "Don't worry about me. I'll be right behind you."

They caught a cab home at Northern Boulevard. They quickly opened the door, rushed inside, and bolted the heavy locks on the new steel door. "Are you going to call the detective now?" Julianna asked.

"No. I think I'll handle this myself. It's time I put an end to this."

He went down, opened his safe, and took out the Beretta M-09 that he used during his stint in Iraq and Afghanistan. Eddie kept his gun locked in the safe because of the ridiculous New York City gun laws that prohibited a homeowner from protecting himself against an intruder. He brought it upstairs, laid it on the table and field stripped it in a matter of seconds. He proceeded to clean and oil it, then he loaded 9mm rounds into the two clips. He inserted one clip into the gun and placed it under his belt, where he could get at it in a hurry. Eddie knew it was either him or them and, if he had Claiborne figured right, the man was crazy. He wouldn't stop coming after him until one of them was dead. Well, Eddie had played this game before when he was in the service.

He never figured he'd have to become that man again, but he had no choice. Only Claiborne would be the one to pay, not him.

Eddie went to a trunk he kept in the bedroom and removed clothes until he reached the bottom. He smiled as he pulled out the neatly folded black Delta combat uniform he kept as a souvenir, and as a reminder that he had once been a soldier. He swapped his clothes for the Delta clothing that he hadn't worn in years. He was pleased it still fit him perfectly.

When he came back upstairs, Julianna didn't recognize the man she had just married. He looked like a ghost, a menacing apparition of death and, for a moment, he frightened her. This was a side of Eddie she had never seen before.

"What are you going to do, Eddie?"

"I'm sure they're out there somewhere. I'll find them and put an end to this nightmare."

"Eddie, please don't go out there. I'm afraid they'll kill you."

Eddie smiled, his teeth shining brightly within his darkened face. He embraced his wife and whispered softly in her ear, "Don't you worry about me; this is my game they're playing now, and I'm better at it than they are. If they're out there, I'll find them."

"And if they're not?"

"Then I'll be back and we'll do it again tomorrow night."

Eddie left through the back door and made his way up the alley, hidden by the hour of the night and aided by his friend the darkness, where the shadows kept him invisible. He cautiously looked up and down the block. He was surprised at how quickly his training took over and how easily he slipped back into being a soldier. There was movement to his left on the corner, and it was clear to him that it wasn't a local resident. Two men walked silently and quickly toward his house, trying to keep in the shadows. Eddie lay in the prone position alongside some garbage pails no more than ten feet from where they came to a halt. He listened to Claiborne give instructions to his gunman. "Go around to the back and see if there's a way in. If there is, come back here and we'll go in together. I'll see if I can get in through one of the windows. Calto has installed a steel door and I'm sure it has heavy security measures built into it. Listen up. This guy has a sophisticated alarm system, so as soon as we get in, we have to kill him and get out fast before the police arrive."

His associate turned to him before leaving. "Look, you're paying me a lot of money to do this for you, but what I don't get is why are you doing it if you're not taking anything from the guy? I can see you whacking the guy then stealing his money or jewels or something, but I don't understand why you're taking a chance like this and getting nothing out of it."

Claiborne smiled malevolently. "What I'm getting out of this, Otto, is revenge. That's what I'm taking from him— revenge. Kill his wife first, so he sees it."

Otto was a hard man, but he was getting a little nervous just being near Claiborne. When he took the job, he hadn't realized how unbalanced the man was. He had a bad feeling about this job and, if he had his way, he'd just walk away from it. Otto had never taken a job where the risk was great and nothing was gained from the contract. Even if his job was to murder someone, somebody benefitted from it one way or another, but this job tonight was crazy, almost as crazy as Claiborne. Otto was hired to kill a husband and now he was told he must kill the wife too? Nothing would come from taking the contract other than seeing this crazy fool happy about his revenge. "You know what, Claiborne. I don't think I want to do this. Killing a woman was never part of the deal. I never killed a woman before and I don't want to start now."

"What? What do you mean, you don't want to do this? I paid you a lot of money to kill Calto and his wife."

"You paid me a lot of money to kill Calto. His wife was never part of the deal."

Claiborne stammered for a moment. "Look, I'm not going to stand here arguing with you all night. All right. I'll double what I'm paying you if you kill the girl too."

Otto shook his head, while staring defiantly at Claiborne. "You don't listen very well. I told you I never killed a woman before and I won't start now. Look, I'm not a nice guy. I rob people and I kill people for money, but I have two rules, which are 1. I don't kill children, and 2. I don't kill women. I've lived by those rules and I'm not going to break them for you or anyone else. Got that?"

Claiborne was furious. If he hadn't reacted, he might have thought better of it. But instead of thinking he reacted on instinct. He shot Otto. But as Otto was driven back by the bullet, he fired a shot at Claiborne, hitting him in the center of his forehead and killing him before he hit the ground. Eddie waited for a moment to make sure Claiborne's was dead, then looked at the other man. The man was down and he wasn't moving. One look at Claiborne and Eddie knew he was dead;

so he left Claiborne's gun where he dropped it and went to Otto to check his wound.

Otto grimaced as he looked up at him then smiled grimly. "You were there all the time listening, weren't you?"

"Yeah."

"You heard everything?"

"Yeah, I heard everything."

Otto gasped for breath. "Look, it wasn't personal. It was just business."

Eddie patted him on the shoulder. "I know. Can you stand?"

"I don't know. I don't think so."

"Come on, I'll help you up. I want to get you in the house and see how badly you're hurt."

"Why? Why are you helping me?"

"Well, when I was in the service, sometimes we had to take out one of the bad guys and that was nothing personal. It was just business. I look at what you were going to do tonight as something like what I did at times in the war, and I don't hold that against you. Maybe it's because you never got to finish the job, or maybe it's because you wouldn't agree to harm my wife, or maybe it's because it's over. It is over, isn't it?"

Otto managed to nod his head a few times. "Yeah, it's over. I never felt right about this job to begin with."

Eddie banged on the door with his free arm while he held up Otto with the other. "Julianna, it's me, Eddie. Open the door."

Julianna opened the door. Her hand went to her lips and she gasped as she saw the blood-drenched shirt on the wounded man.

"Let's get him inside and clean him up," Eddie said. "I want to see how bad his wound is."

With some difficulty Eddie managed to take off Otto's jacket. "Julianna, get a blanket and lay it over the couch. I want to lay him down there and tend to his wound." With the blanket spread over the couch and with Julianna's help, they laid Otto on the couch. Eddie bent over, opened Otto's shirt, and saw where the bullet had entered the lower part of his abdomen. "I'm gonna turn you around so I can see if the bullet passed through or if it's still inside you." When Eddie turned Otto over, he saw a small protrusion in his back. The bullet hadn't quite passed through. "Well, the bullet's still in you, but if you're up to it, I think I can get it out."

Otto looked up at him. "You mean you can cut it out of me, don't you?"

"Yeah! It's just about out; but, if you want, we can wait for the medics to get here and they'll take you to the hospital and remove the bullet there."

"Have you ever done anything like this before?"

"No, not like this, but I had friends of mine who were wounded, so I'm not a complete stranger to this. I know what has to be done. Besides, my wife here is a nurse and she can take care of you after I get the bullet out."

Otto gritted his teeth and managed a tight-lipped smile. "Go ahead and do it, but do it fast, all right?"

Eddie took out his stainless steel tactical knife, which he always kept razor sharp. He lit the stove and put the blade over the flame for a few seconds, then opened the faucet and doused the blade under the cold water to cool it off. "Julianna, get me a clean dishtowel and bring it here, please. Good. Now hold it under here." He pointed to a spot under the protrusion. "Good. Now keep it there. Hold on now; this won't take but a second." Eddie cut a small incision about a quarter of an inch long, pressed the flesh on either side, and watched as the bullet squeezed out and dropped into the towel. Julianna swabbed some iodine into the wound and put a Band-Aid over it to keep it clean.

"I don't think the bullet hit any vital organs, but you should have a doctor look at it. Now, can you sit up?" she asked.

"Yeah, with a little help, I can."

Eddie helped Otto sit up. "Are you feeling all right?"

"Yeah I got a little dizzy there for a moment, but I'm okay."

"Try standing."

Eddie helped Otto stand and, once he was on his feet, he managed to remain upright as another bout of dizziness passed. Otto looked at Eddie with a confused expression. "What do we do now?"

"Well, I'm going to call the police now. I have a dead man outside my home and someone has to remove the garbage."

"But what are you going to do about me?"

"As long as I have your word you'll never bother me or my wife again, I'm gonna let you go. I'll tell the police I heard some gunshots and when I went out to look, Claiborne was dead and I didn't see who killed him."

"Do you have a pencil and a piece of paper?" The question confused Eddie, but he went to the desk drawer and returned with both. Otto wrote something on the paper. "Here, keep this somewhere safe. It's a number where I can be reached. Just tell the man who answers that you have to talk to me and he'll take your number. He'll see to it that I get it and I'll return your call. You see, Calto, not only do you have my word that I won't ever harm you or your wife, but you also have my word that if you ever need anything, you call that number and I will help you. I owe you big time for what you've done for me tonight, and Otto doesn't forget his obligations."

"I'll help you to your car."

"No. Call the police before someone spots the body and does it for you. I'm feeling much better now."

Eddie and Julianna watched a wounded Otto hobble down the street to his car. When he drove away, Eddie called the police and took a quick shower to wash the camouflage from his face. He put on casual clothes while Julianna took the bloody blanket off the couch, put it in a laundry bag and laid some towels over it. Eddie would get rid of it tomorrow.

"What an anti-climax this was," he said "I got all dressed in my combat outfit and was ready to kill two men and all I wound up doing was watch you put a Band-Aid on a bad guy."

Julianna laughed and poured them coffee. Then they sat down on the couch, turned on the TV, and waited for the police to arrive.

Chapter 36

Detective McGovern sat drumming his fingers on the kitchen table. Eddie told him everything that happened except the part about taking care of Otto's gunshot wound and letting him go. When he finished explaining, the detective asked a simple question. "How do you explain the bloodstains leading to your door?"

Eddie turned to Julianna. "So that was the knocking we heard on the door." Eddie looked McGovern in the eye. "Let me get this straight. A wounded man knocked on my door because he was looking to finish the job he was hired to do— and that was to kill me? Is that what you're suggesting, Detective?"

McGovern scratched his head. It did sound kind of silly, especially hearing Eddie tell it that way.

"Or maybe you're thinking I opened the door, let the guy in, then killed him and buried him somewhere in the house."

McGovern waved his hand, dismissing such a foolish notion. "No, that's not what I'm saying."

"Wait a minute," Eddie said. "I got it. I heard the knock on the door. I opened it and welcomed the bad guy in. Then I saw that he was wounded, so I patched him up and sent him on his way. That's it, right, Detective. Is that what you think I might've done?"

McGovern scrunched his eyes and waved his hand once again. "No, no, no, that's not what I mean. Damn, but this is getting confusing. I have bloodstains leading from Claiborne's body to your front door. Then the bloodstains stop. I know this much. Claiborne and another man shot it out and Claiborne

207

was killed; but before he died, he shot and wounded the guy that shot him. Then the wounded man disappeared into thin air."

"You're looking at it all wrong, Lieutenant. Claiborne and another man shot it out and Claiborne was killed, and we know that he wounded the other man. The wounded man walked to my home and knocked on the door and, when I didn't answer it, he turned and walked away. But he realized he was losing too much blood, so he tied his arm or leg or whatever to stop his blood loss. And with that done, he walked to his car and drove away. That makes more sense to me than conjuring up all sorts of scenarios that won't work."

"Yeah, I guess you're right. I'll write my report, stating there was a gunfight where one man was killed and the other man, although presumed to be wounded, managed to escape. In any case, you won't have to worry about Claiborne coming after you any longer, and the wounded guy won't come after you because there's nothing in it for him. Now you can go on with the rest of your life without having to look over your shoulder, wondering if someone is going to hurt you. You two are pretty famous now, so why don't you take a trip somewhere and enjoy your fifteen minutes of fame."

Eddie put his arm around the cop and, just as he walked him to the door, the telephone rang. He was about to answer it, but turned to his wife. "Julianna, can you get that for me please. You know, McGovern, it's too bad we won't be seeing each other again. I was beginning to take a liking to you and this could have been the beginning of a beautiful friendship."

McGovern laughed. "You watched *Casablanca* too, eh? You know, kid, all kidding aside, you're beginning to grow a little on me too. See ya around."

When Eddie returned to the kitchen, Julianna rushed over to him and put her arms around him as tears welled in her eyes. He grabbed her gently by her shoulders. "What happened? What's wrong? Why are you crying?"

"Oh, Eddie," she said between sobs. "I've never been so happy in my life. That phone call was from our lawyer. He just left a meeting with the City of New Orleans' attorneys and the city has acknowledged the validity of the deeds. Since the deeds were proven to be valid, the city had no choice but to negotiate a settlement."

"And?" Eddie asked anxiously.

"And the city of New Orleans has agreed to settle the law suit for eight billion dollars."

©Black Horse Publishing

For more about the author, future novels, and events, please visit.
WWW.CORSOBOOKS.COM

If you enjoyed this story, please leave a review about your experience.

All of Joe Corso's books are available online.

The Time Portal Series
The Old Man and the King
The Starlight Club Series
The Revenge of John W
The Adventures of the Lone Jack Kid
The Comeback
Engine 24: Fire Stories

An Invitation to Book Clubs

I would like to extend an invitation to book club members across the country. Invite me to your book club and I will be happy to join in your discussion. I am available to join your discussion via phone (speaker), online (via discussion board or Skype), in person, or by any other means. You may arrange a day or time by contacting me at corsobooks@yahoo.com. I look forward to hearing from you.

31515495R00129

Made in the USA
Charleston, SC
19 July 2014